Rosemary Allison.

THE SPANISH LADY

Charles Connell feels safe in asking Harry Warrender to accompany him on an unorthodox trip to Spain, for they had been boys together and Harry has resource and know-how. They are to bring back the last of the Mundaya family treasures. Luis Mundaya, a vigorous opponent of the Franco government, has been a political prisoner for years and his daughter Isabella has made her home in England.

They reach Spain in good order, meet Isabella and her father, and prepare to carry out their task. But during one tragic night of action in a remote hill district of Santander Harry's true character emerges. Luis Mundaya dies, Charles is gravely wounded, and Harry vanishes with treasures worth £30,000; the three paintings by Zubaran of " The Spanish Lady."

The final scene of Mr. Cronin's gripping new novel is played out in London, where Harry hopes to turn the paintings to his own profit. But he has some surprises awaiting him.

THE
SPANISH LADY

by

MICHAEL CRONIN

ROBERT HALE LIMITED
63 Old Brompton Road London S.W.7

PRINTED IN GREAT BRITAIN BY
BRISTOL TYPESETTING CO. LTD.
STOKES CROFT   -   BRISTOL

PART ONE

"PREPARING"

1

W HEN CHARLES CONNELL decided that Harry Warrender was the man he needed—and he could think of nobody else who might be of the slightest use for what he had in mind—he spent over a week looking for him in the pubs and clubs and similar spots in what he knew to be Harry's district.

They hadn't met for some four or five months, but Connell didn't imagine that Harry had changed his habits. He followed up a number of dud clues and drank a lot of unwanted liquor in a variety of places in the course of his search.

Harry's circle of acquaintances was a wide one and a very mixed one, and some members of it were prepared to be coy about Harry's whereabouts, more on general principles than for any other reason, which did not expedite the search.

One or two who remembered having seen Charles Connell with Harry and who thus assumed that the enquiry might be legitimate without being legal, and possibly, as Connell hinted, to Harry's benefit, admitted that Harry hadn't been seen around the area recently; he was either short of money or in trouble over a woman; or both.

Harry Warrender was in the middle thirties but looked rather older; he was a big expansive man with heavy shoulders, an impressive high-coloured face, and a thick dark moustache that gave him a military spruceness; he had the unashamed beginnings of a paunch, beer-induced.

Charles Connell had known him since boyhood, and they had kept in touch, off and on, ever since; their careers had been totally dissimilar, which was probably the reason why they could still meet.

At one time Harry had held a regular commission in R.E.M.E., and there was still a good deal of the military in his bearing; his premature return to civil life was not a topic upon which he was ever very forthcoming, but Connell had understood from Harry in one of his few unguarded drunken moments that he had failed to agree with the Army Council concerning the handling of certain trifling Mess funds.

Harry was a first class mechanical engineer and a superlatively good driver; in his better days he had done well in the Mille Miglia and had been respectably placed several times in the Monte Carlo Rally. He ought to have been comfortably positioned somewhere in the automobile industry, and had in fact held one or two responsible appointments for varying lengths of time.

But something always went wrong and Harry would be at liberty again; the simple truth was that he disliked regular hours of work, and liked to be able to take a couple of days off or a longish weekend whenever he felt like it. Also an elastic lunch interval was essential to the successful cultivation of Harry's contacts, mostly feminine. Thus very few boards of directors availed themselves of Harry's services for very long.

Harry's progress downwards was inevitable, yet he retained an enormous gusto for life and was eternally optimistic about the future. He had been married once, early on, to a well-bred girl who had mistaken his easy charm and superficial energy for more sterling qualities; she soon went back to mother, and the divorce followed.

In the course of the last year Harry had been involved in a number of ' deals ' that produced a precarious reward and necessitated some hurried trips out of London and an amount of monosyllabic telephoning at the most unseasonable hours of the day and night.

Charles Connell had no doubt that a number of these alleged ' deals ' would not stand examination. Harry had become a plausible rogue and he was quite happy about himself, as far as one could judge.

Connell's own career had been vastly different; after qualifying as an architect he had joined his father in a prosperous Surrey ' dormitory '; by unflagging application to the job, and by developing an unsuspected flair for handling wealthy clients he had raised the firm's prestige to the point where his father had become little more than a sleeping partner.

Charles Connell had never married, for many years he said he was too busy to bother; the one or two tentative approaches he had made towards suitable girls had come to nothing because of his basic lack of curiosity about and interest in women. Harry Warrender, from his vast and continuing experience, made a comic business of this and from time to time offered Charles all manner of improper assistance.

To Harry it didn't make much sense : Charles wasn't a ' queer ', he had money and was likely to have a lot more, he wasn't too bad to look at if you didn't mind the skinny intense type—all in all he ought to make some girl a good husband. Harry found shyness about women very funny indeed.

Charles Connell finally came up with him in the saloon bar of a small pub in Maida Vale. Harry had a girl with him, naturally, but she was most assuredly not the reason for his recent withdrawal from circulation.

She was about eighteen and she wore tight tartan pants and a not very clean pale blue jersey; her breasts were rather too heavy for the rest of her; she had untidy indeterminate blonde hair and she looked very sulky as though life had temporarily gone back on her; she squatted on a tall stool with her feet curled around its legs; she was drinking tomato juice with the expression of one who hasn't said anything for a long time and intended to keep it like that; she was considerably younger than the kind of woman Harry normally spent his time with: he liked them to be in the late twenties, old enough to know the way around but still young enough to be enthusiastic.

Harry himself was wearing a shaggy mustard-and-green tweed suit that made him look bigger than ever. The elbows of the jacket were reinforced with patches of bright brown leather and he still wore one of the striped Old Boys ties that Charles Connell had given up wearing years ago. His thick black hair had begun to recede in front. With his hand clamped around a pint tankard and his heavy shoulders spreading against the seams of his jacket he was in soft earnest conversation with the barman: wherever he went Harry always seemed to find a common bond with the men who stood behind bar counters—as he said himself, one day perhaps he'd finish up there himself.

As Connell came in Harry saw him in the mirror over the bar, put down his tankard, and said:

" Stone the crows, if it isn't old Charles!"

The rest of his welcome was equally hearty and nobody

else in the saloon could remain unaware of the fact that Harry had met an old friend.

The girl in the tartan pants was introduced as Susie. She nodded and contributed nothing to the gaiety of the occasion; she gave Charles Connell a slow examination and apparently came to the conclusion that he was one friend of Harry's she could do without.

Harry ordered up drinks with his customary heartiness and there was the usual banter when Charles Connell protested that all he wanted was a half pint; Harry liked to pretend that nothing less than a pint was worth lifting off the counter.

The girl soon left. She just unwound her feet from the stool, tugged those tight pants down more firmly over her small hips, and said flatly : " See you, Harry."

" We'll do that, sweetie." Harry absently turned and watched her go out as though wondering who she was. " Nice kid," he said automatically. They were all nice kids, even when they turned him down.

" I hope I didn't drive her away," Connell said, " I didn't mean to break up anything, Harry."

" Forget it. I was only passing the time. Now we can get down to some serious drinking. I forgot—how's the ulcer these days ?"

" Fair," said Connell. " I watch it." He had done no more than taste his beer.

" Tough," said Harry. " You work too hard and you worry too much, Charles—that's what. Ought to be like me. Not a care in the world."

He lifted his tankard and drank by way of demonstrating his defiance of fate and tomorrow's headaches. The cuff of his shirt was frayed and none too clean. He put down his drink and gave himself a resounding slap in the belly, one of his invariable drinking gestures, indicating satisfaction with himself and his immediate surroundings. The pouches under his watery blue eyes had become more pronounced since Charles Connell had last seen him.

Seedy was the word for Harry.

"You've proved very elusive," Connell said. "I've been looking all over the place for you. Nobody seemed to know where you were."

"Well now," said Harry, "I've been around, Charles, here and there." His eyes had sharpened a little, almost as though Charles had been one of the concourse to whom he owed money. "I keep pretty busy."

"That's fine," said Connell. "I'm very glad to hear it."

"Oh yes," said Harry Warrender, "things are moving." Anyone who didn't know him might imagine all manner of glittering opportunities about to fall into Harry's lap.

"Good." Charles Connell's dark flannel suit seemed to accentuate his thinness. He wasn't at home in that bar and Harry's colourful flamboyance made it all the more evident.

"So you didn't just walk in here by accident—I ought to be flattered, Charles."

Harry wondered, and not for the first time, just how much Charles was worth; he had done some big jobs in the last six or seven years.

One odd feature about their long friendship was that Harry had never tried to borrow money from Charles, and at one time or another Harry had borrowed from most people who saw much of him.

The way Harry saw it, if he borrowed from Charles it would upset the whole balance between them; as it was, Charles was the only man of substance whom he could still meet on equal terms. And that continued to help Harry's belief that things were all right with Harry.

Another thing was that Harry never really envied his friend's prosperity : he was enough of a realist to know that he could never have been the kind of man Charles had become; even at school Charles had always been ready to work and do without things.

They had known each other so long, they met at irregular intervals, and Harry still felt he got more fun out of life than Charles did. He began to give a colourful and scandalous account of his own proceedings in the last few months, adding all the embroidery Charles had come to expect. The pints went down with an absent-minded fluency, while Charles still played with his first modest drink and went on waiting while the words flowed over him and Harry eventually reached the inevitable stage of boyhood reminiscence and the good old days.

After that there was lunch, a meal Harry was quite ready to skip, but Charles insisted because of the gastric ulcer.

After they had finished eating Charles Connell said :

" Harry, are you tied up with anything important in the next few weeks? Anything you couldn't put off for a bit ?"

Harry Warrender reflected, his red face shining after food and plenty of drink. " Well," he said carefully, " I have a number of propositions I'm considering—they aren't all important, though—some of them wouldn't spoil. What's on your mind, Charles ?"

" I've got something," Charles Connell said slowly. " Something I want to do—and I don't think I can do it by myself—it's rather out of my line."

Harry took a cigarette from the open case between them. For the first time that he could remember Charles wanted something from him, and wanted it badly enough to come looking for him. " If it's out of your line you think it might fit me. That's interesting, Charles—I don't draw a terribly thick line myself these days, and you know it."

Charles Connell was shifting the remnants of the cutlery about, lining up spoons and forks in his thin deft fingers. His narrow face with the high cheekbones was thoughtful.

" It could be a tricky business," he said.

" So you thought of me." Harry smiled. " Don't tell me you've got trouble on your mind, not you, Charles—I just don't believe it could be as serious as you look."

" I wish I knew how to put it properly." Charles Connell brushed the cutlery to one side. " Harry, would you be willing to come to Spain with me on a private job? It would be worth a couple of hundred to you and all expenses."

Harry Warrender laughed, a little bitterly. " Is that what you were so shy about? The way things are with me I'd postpone my grannie's funeral for half that much. A private job, Charles—and nothing to do with architecture. Am I right?"

Connell nodded. " It won't be any ordinary trip."

" Naturally. Not for two hundred pounds." Harry Warrender's pale blue eyes were intelligent, and a little amused perhaps. He was no stranger to off-colour propositions: Charles was as uneasy as hell; this wasn't his kind of thing at all.

Charles looked across at him. " You mightn't like it when I give you the details."

" They'd need to be very rough before I'd turn them down. Let's be a little more specific, Charles, shall we? I'm fairly shock-proof."

" There is an element of risk involved," said Charles in a careful voice. " I have to tell you that."

" I didn't expect anything else, not at the price you offer." Harry shot his cuffs and rested his chin on his clenched fists; the thick black hair curled on the backs of his hands and wrists; he radiated strength and confidence.

" Risk," he repeated softly. " Now I wonder about that: was I the only one you knew sufficiently lacking in scruples? You interest me, Charles."

" I didn't mean it like that." Charles Connell shook his head.

Harry Warrender was smiling. " I don't insult all that easily these days. When do we talk about it?"

Charles Connell looked around the crowded restaurant. " Not here."

" There's my place," said Harry. " It isn't very special but we wouldn't be interrupted."

They drove back to Kilburn; Harry was in an aluminium and blue Austin Special that was far too small for one of his build; he explained that he was looking after it for a friend; in recent years Harry seldom seemed to own the cars he drove and very infrequently appeared in successive weeks in the same car—and all of them were in the process of being sold; according to Harry the Austin was a real snip at sixty pounds for any sporty lad who wanted to give his girl a treat, so long as the girl didn't expect doors and a windscreen.

Under Harry's skilful handling the Austin showed surprising acceleration and its exhaust crackled with blue smoke. Charles Connell followed respectably in his black Rover 90.

Harry had two rooms on the first floor of an old Victorian building behind Kilburn High Road. A coffee-coloured youth in a pink shirt and washed-out khaki jeans was squatting on the front steps.

" Hi, Harry," he said lazily. " Some day soon you break that l'il pram, man."

Harry good-naturedly cuffed the side of his head and told him to belt up. Charles Connell was remembering the days when Harry had a smart service flat with a porter in a green uniform; Harry's better addresses had always been quite impressive. He followed Harry up the dark stairs.

The living-room had a small sink in one corner and a miniature gas stove behind a screen; the bright afternoon sun showed up the shabbiness of the furniture and the faded patches on the wall where pictures had hung; the door into the bedroom was open, the double bed hadn't been made and there was a woman's bedroom slipper lying by the foot of the bed; there was a smell of stale face powder about the whole place.

" Convenient and cheap," said Harry Warrender briefly. He picked up a nylon stocking from one of the tattered armchairs, rolled it into a ball in his large fists and stuffed it into his pocket. He wasn't embarrassed. He smiled at Charles Connell and said: " She left last night and I haven't had time to clear up—she won't be back. Have a seat, Charles."

He went behind the screen and came back with a quart bottle of light ale and two glasses.

" Not for me, thanks," said Connell. " You go ahead."

Harry poured himself a glass, held it up to the light and said: " Cheers for both of us." He emptied the glass in one controlled unbroken tilt of his arm with his eyes closed reverently. He put the glass down. " That's a lot better. Now, Charles, you tell me about Spain."

2

"I want you to come to Spain with me and help me to get something out. Some pictures, Harry."

Harry Warrender poured himself some more light ale, watching the thin white froth creep up inside the glass as though it had a cash value all of its own.

"We'd have to do it under cover," said Connell.

"The word you want is smuggle. Right?"

Charles Connell nodded. Harry lit a cigarette; he was sitting with his heavy thighs apart.

"You surprise me, Charles," he said. "I didn't think you had it in you."

"It's illegal. But there are special circumstances."

Harry smiled. "They must be very special, to have you involved—I doubt if you've ever sneaked anything much past the customs. I take it this is a big job?"

"It is." Charles Connell looked down at the polished toe caps of his shoes and then across at Harry's broad smiling face.

"Go on," said Harry.

"As I told you, it isn't quite my kind of thing, but whether you come in with me or not I'm going to have a shot at it."

Harry Warrender gave himself a cigarette. "Lots of people smuggle," he said mildly, "and nobody feels terribly guilty about it—unless they get caught. Whose pictures are these, Charles?"

Charles Connell was silent for a moment. "Harry, it's a complicated story—and it involves other people."

Harry knuckled his moustache. "And you're wondering how far you're going to have to trust me. A difficult situation for you, Charles—at this stage there isn't much I can do for you, not until I know a hell of a lot more." He was smiling. "You want some help getting some pictures out of Spain. All right, I'm interested. You go on from there. You came looking for me because you thought I could help you."

"I'm sorry, Harry," said Connell, "that sounded pretty raw. I didn't quite mean it like that—I wasn't being cagey—just clumsy. Did you ever hear me talk about the Mundaya family?"

"Maybe. Friends of your father's, in Spain—didn't you spend a holiday with them once when you were at school? I seem to remember being very envious at the time—my folks took me to Clacton."

"Luis Mundaya and my father have been friends for many years," said Connell, "ever since Mundaya was at Cambridge. In fact, Mundaya eventually married a distant cousin on my mother's side of the family—it caused quite a bother back home in Spain: the Mundayas were a wealthy and influential family with estates in Asturias and Santander: very Spanish and very proud. They didn't think much of this marriage to an unknown and unimportant English girl. It just wasn't the right thing at all. From what I've heard of him from my father Lius Mundaya never fitted into the family pattern—he was always a bit of a rebel. He read Law at Cambridge, and he was expected to go back home to Spain and marry according to the family plan. You can imagine the kind of thing: a nice Spanish Catholic girl of a good family with a dowry and all the rest of it. I believe they had the girl already picked out and willing."

Charles Connell paused and took out his handkerchief and mopped his brow, a little fussily.

"Sorry," said Harry. He got up and threw the window open. "Not exactly air-conditioned." In the house opposite somebody was learning the guitar and showing little talent for it.

Charles Connell shoved his chair back out of the sunshine. Harry Warrender slowly drank some beer.

"Needs ice," he said. And then: "So Luis Mundaya brought his English bride home and stirred things up. Very romantic and I hope they were happy."

"They were. Luis Mundaya was the kind of man who flourished on opposition. When the Spanish Civil War started he was on the Government side; in his view Franco was a Fascist, no better than Hitler or Mussolini. Luis wasn't content just to run the family estates and be a cultured Spanish gentleman; he went in for politics very actively—with the family money behind him and the Mundaya name most doors were open to him and he was making a reputation for himself when the fighting started. He didn't see Franco as the cure for Spain's poverty and ignorance and general lethargy. In his heart, like so many other Spaniards, he was—and still is, I think—a monarchist."

"So he's still alive," said Harry. "He must have had some luck. What did he do when his boys lost? Skip the country?"

"He went to jail," said Connell flatly. "When things were obviously going wrong he sent his wife and daughter

back to England. They only had one child. Isabella. She
was brought up in England—her mother died shortly after
they got here : she didn't want to leave Spain and her husband, but Luis wasn't going to take any chances for them.
He didn't mind about himself. It's really because of
Isabella that I'm telling you all this, Harry. She stayed
with us one summer—you probably met her."

"I remember," said Harry Warrender. "A skinny little
kid with long pigtails and a hell of a temper."

Charles smiled. "Well, the description doesn't exactly
fit now."

"They grow up," said Harry. "I know."

"You can judge for yourself when you see her." Connell's voice was careful. "Some people might call her
beautiful."

"Good. I look forward to it. But what happened to her
father?"

"They kept him in jail for a number of years. His
property was confiscated. He probably would have been
shot but for the intervention of the rest of the Mundaya
clan. They supported the Falange and they must have had
some pull with Franco's government; at all events, they
managed to save Luis from a firing squad but they couldn't
stop him being stripped of his property—I don't imagine
they tried very hard, at least, that's what Isabella says, and
she ought to know. She spent a lot of time in Spain trying
to get her father released, pestering the authorities and the
Embassy—she even tried to get an interview with Franco
himself but it didn't quite come off. She's an unusual girl."

"So I gather. Guts and good looks : a nice combination.
The pictures you spoke about : would they be part of the
Mundaya property that didn't happen to get confiscated?"

Charles Connell nodded. "They belonged to Luis—you

might say they still do. I told you there were special circumstances, Harry. They're all he has left. He's an old man
now, pretty sick—they let him out four months ago. He had
a few short periods of freedom before, but he made no
attempt to hide what he felt about the regime: to him it
was still a corrupt dictatorship. Isabella with the help of
some of his friends tried to get him to leave the country
and come to England, but he wouldn't. He was a Spaniard
and Spain was his country and he wasn't going to let himself be driven out by a gang of plunderers and Fascists. So
they put him back behind bars again—it was the only way
to shut him up and keep him out of their hair. I imagine
they regretted they didn't shoot him years ago."

"I begin to see where his daughter gets her spirit from,"
said Harry Warrender.

"Yes, she's very like her father, I suppose. Certainly
she's devoted to him; she won't listen to any criticism of
him, and you can imagine what the other Mundayas and
their respectable family connections thought about Luis.
To Isabella her father is a hero, just about the best ever.
They let him out of prison about four months ago and if he
goes back again it'll be the end of him, I think: plenty of
Spanish jails aren't all that special, at least not for a man
over sixty with one lung gone and crippled with arthritis.
He's been staying on a small farm up in the hills about
twenty miles from Santander; the farm belongs to one of
his old tenants—Luis won't have anything to do with the
other members of his family; it would suit them of course if
Isabella could persuade him to leave the country, but he
refuses to go. He's in poor shape but they can't talk him
into anything he doesn't want to do, and being heaved out
of his own country is one of them. Besides, there are the
pictures."

As he listened Harry Warrender had gradually slid down in his chair; Charles was being so earnest and careful about his story. Harry thrust his powerful legs out in front of him. There wasn't much of the light ale left. The guitar player across the road was plunking away indomitably.

"The pictures," Harry repeated. "I've been wondering when we'd come to them."

Charles Connell made a brief gesture with one hand. "I wanted you to know the full circumstances—this isn't any ordinary job—I don't imagine I'd be interested in it myself if I didn't know Isabella."

Harry Warrender smiled. "You've done pretty well so far. She must be rather a special girl."

"She is. Harry, there are three paintings hidden in a country house that used to belong to Luis Mundaya: Luis put them there just before he was arrested and sent to prison for the first time; the Mundayas have always been patrons of the arts and these three paintings were the most valuable in the collection. They are by Zurbaran, not very big, but together they're worth about thirty thousand pounds."

Slowly Harry Warrender came upright. "You surprise me."

"I said it was a big job. The paintings have never been discovered; Isabella didn't know about them herself until her father was let out of prison this time—he told her what he had done and ever since then she's been trying to think up ways of getting the pictures out—the tricky part is that the house and the estate were given to a man named Carceres, Juan Carceres, for services to the Franco government; Luis Mundaya was interrogated in prison about the paintings—genuine Zurbarans aren't all that common—but Luis wouldn't tell them anything."

"So it will require a little burglary as well. It begins to build up, Charles—I'm still interested. But tell me, will Isabella Mundaya ever be able to sell these paintings? I imagine they'll be known to collectors all over the world."

"Isabella has a buyer all ready. There's a millionaire from Argentina who knows pretty well all about them : his father was a tenant farmer of the Mundayas and he takes the same view as Isabella and Luis Mundaya : the paintings are Mundaya property and an edict of confiscation by the Franco government doesn't worry him at all—if Isabella can deliver the pictures to him in good condition he may be willing to go as high as thirty-five thousand. He's a powerful man and he's up to all the financial dodges—the idea is for him to arrange funds for Luis Mundaya in Spain so that he can live out the rest of his days in reasonable comfort : at present he's living like a peasant and he won't accept any help from relatives—his presence in Spain rather embarrasses them, I expect : they don't like being reminded that at least one member of the family was on the losing side. Isabella has been working for a travel agency here in London; she wanted to stay with her father when they let him out of prison but it was obvious that they wouldn't be able to do anything about the paintings if she stayed in Spain. Luis told her about Menendez from the Argentine as a possible buyer if they ever got the pictures out; Joachim Menendez made his money after the first World War and when he came back to Spain as a wealthy visitor he met Luis Mundaya and made an offer for the Zurbarans : I suppose it gave him a bit of a boost to be making an offer for the treasured possessions of the man who used to be his father's lord and master. Isabella got in touch with him and met him in London a week ago; he's still interested and he'll be at the Dorchester most of the summer."

" That seems to take care of that end of it." Harry Warrender folded his hands across his paunch. He looked a
little sleepy. " And this dollar-loaded Argentinian won't
be asking any difficult questions."

" He wants the Zurbarans. As far as he is concerned they
belong to Luis Mundaya : all he wants is for them to be
delivered to him. He knows Luis Mundaya's circumstances."

" So all we have to do is to get the pictures out. It begins
to sound like quite a chore."

" It can be done. It needs planning. And two men. I
hoped you'd be one of them, Harry." Charles Connell's
voice had become a little edgy, almost uncomfortable.
" Isabella didn't want to tell me about it, but I knew something was worrying her and I got it out of her in the end;
she's been staying with my sister at weekends—I think she
had some crazy notion of trying to smuggle the pictures out
on her own—so of course I told her she could count on
me."

" Naturally." Harry Warrender's voice was flat, careful,
committing him to nothing. " And so you came along to
see old Harry and here we are. It needs thinking about,
Charles."

" If it's the money," said Charles Connell quickly, " it
might be possible to arrange for three hundred."

" I take it you are financing the deal at this stage. It must
be nice to be able to be so chivalrous."

Charles Connell stood up. " I made a mistake. I'm sorry
I bothered you, Harry."

" For Pete's sake sit down," said Warrender, " and don't
be so damned gentlemanly. If you go off half-cock on this
thing just because I made an off-side comment you certainly
won't do old Mundaya any good. Or the resourceful Isa-

bella." He smiled. " Put it down to the company I've been keeping lately. All right : this is a business deal, you are putting up the funds. You think I can help you. So far : fine. I'm with you. Now tell me about these paintings that are worth so much money. How big are they?"

Connell sat down again. " I'm a bit jumpy," he said. " I've been trying to plan this thing and I haven't got very far. The paintings are about two foot square each, and they mustn't be rolled, at least, Luis Mundaya says it would be dangerous and might ruin them—crack the paint or spoil the canvas I suppose—they'll have to travel flat, and in some kind of a container."

" Well, there's the first snag," said Warrender quite cheerfully. " That rules out any chance of getting them out with personal luggage : if we packed them in a trunk we might as well kiss them goodbye. So it means a vehicle, suitably modified, Charles—and I'm just the boy for that." He slowly rubbed his hands together. " Not a commercial body and not a saloon. Plenty of room in the back."

" There's my father's Humber, the utility, the one he drove the surveyors around in with all their clobber. It's a heavy old job and he doesn't use it now."

" Could be," said Warrender thoughtfully. " When can I see it?"

Charles Connell stood up again. " Why not now? If you've got the time—?"

Harry Warrender got to his feet, smiling. He patted Connell on the shoulder. " You've got yourself a partner : my time is yours."

3

CHARLES CONNELL still lived with his father in a spacious red-bricked Edwardian villa on the banks of the River Wey just above its junction with the Thames; it was a quiet comfortable riverside house, not at all beautiful or smart; it suggested family punting parties on sunlit afternoons when the new motor racing was all the rage at Brooklands —flannels and striped blazers and spreading muslin frocks under sunshades and tea on the lawn by the water—

Mrs. Connell had been dead for some years and a housekeeper ran the house; Felicity, Charles Connell's only sister, was married to a doctor and lived at Hampton Court; she and Isabella Mundaya had been at school together and still remained close friends.

When Charles Connell and Harry Warrender arrived at the house in the middle of the afternoon Harry Warrender was hoping for a sight of Isabella, but apart from Mrs. Hopton, the housekeeper, there was nobody around; John Connell, Charles's father, was playing golf : his main interest since he had largely retired from active practice.

They went into the wide garage that used to serve as a coach house and stables in the old days. Harry climbed into the Humber; it was a Snipe and the utility body was solid and coach-built with plenty of floor space.

" I think it'll do," he said. He swung his leg over the seat and squatted in the back, testing the floor and examining the corners and the struts that curved down inside the body.

He got out. "She's all right." With surprising agility for one of his build he ducked under the tail-board and crawled underneath the chassis. He emerged, dusted his hands and the knees of his trousers, and said: "I'll have to get it into a workshop, Charles. I think I can fix a false bottom that'll take those pictures. Unless they check the measurements with a foot rule I don't think they'd know the job had been altered—it'll need careful faking, but I can do it. I think I know a small workshop where I can get the right facilities—it'll cost a bit—it's not the sort of job you want to shout about and people have to be paid to keep their mouths shut. Fifty ought to cover it."

Charles Connell nodded. "I'll see how much we have in the safe here. There's beer in the fridge—let's go inside."

Harry Warrender drank a beer in the sitting-room looking out over the long lawn and the river; he was remembering the parties they'd had there years ago: Harry Warrender had been going to do big things in those days.

Charles came back with a long envelope. "I found fifty. If you need more let me know, Harry."

Harry Warrender shot the envelope into the pocket of his jacket. "How much time have we got?"

"Make it as quick as you can. I'll be seeing Isabella this evening—she'll be delighted when she hears."

Harry Warrender was watching Charles Connell's face.

"She's done something to you, Charles," he said. "I've never seen you so full of pep. Are you falling for her?"

"I like her," said Connell stiffly. "I—I admire her courage, and her loyalty to her father."

Harry Warrender was grinning as he looked at his drink.

"Coming from you that's almost a red-hot declaration."

"You're getting the wrong idea, Harry."

"Am I?" Warrender finished his beer quickly. "Can I take the Humber now? I'd like to get started on it over the weekend. I'll get in touch with you in a couple of days and let you know how it's going."

They walked out in the sunshine across the gravel to where the Humber waited. Thoughtfully, his hands in his pockets, Harry Warrender walked all around it like a prospective buyer. "If we can make it look shabby enough we'll get by. I've been thinking, Charles—will Isabella ride with us?"

"No. She'll be there ready when we arrive, with her father."

"Good. We ought to pose as a couple of campers—then we can load up the back with tents and pots and pans and so on. Make it look messy so they won't look too closely. We'll be a couple of open-air types touring the country and we'll have all the right pieces of paper: the A.A. will issue you an International Camping Licence and we can get a list of approved camping sites from the State Tourist Department. The important thing will be for us to look absolutely right and arouse no attention—I'm told that's the only secret to successful evasion of the Customs and other barriers. That and a bit of cheek."

Warrender hitched his trousers over his paunch. "A little nerve goes a long way sometimes." He climbed behind the wheel of the Humber.

Charles Connell thrust his head through the window. "Finding you took a load off my shoulders, Harry—I can't tell you how glad I am. This thing was honestly beyond me on my own."

Harry switched on. " It pays to have a few disreputable friends now and then."

Connell smiled, awkwardly, trying to think of the right thing to say.

" Don't look so stricken with remorse," said Harry cheerfully. " I'm just the boy for this job and we both know it. I'll be in touch with you—tell Isabella the stuff is as good as delivered at the Dorchester."

Charles Connell watched the Humber trundle down the short drive and turn out into the avenue. Harry was really on his uppers; that was clear; but he still had all the bounce in the world, and as he said himself he was the very man a job like this needed : he was tough and resourceful and he knew his way around; Isabella had been uneasy about bringing in a third party and she had needed convincing that to smuggle three very valuable paintings out of Spain was going to require something more than amateur enthusiasm and determination. He had told her about Harry and she had eventually left it to him to decide.

Harry Warrender stopped at Kingston and phoned Striker Lewis. It being four o'clock on a Saturday afternoon Striker was alone at his place of business : a small but very well equipped workshop-cum-garage near Notting Hill; the actual garage was rather larger than it seemed by reason of a concealed entrance to the premises next door for the convenience of repairs that ought not to see the light of day or be visible to any chance visitor.

Striker was over sixty and as spry and as sharp as they come; he had a reasonable volume of legitimate business; the other stuff he took on if it interested him; he was careful and quick and never aimed too high, so he had never had any serious trouble with the police.

Harry Warrender came into the grimy little office; Striker was drinking tea from a blue and white striped beaker, an innocent old hard-working man with gold-rimmed spectacles.

Harry put twenty one-pound notes on the littered desk. " That will rent me a nice quiet little corner in the back room and the use of a few tools. Right ?"

Striker looked out of the window to where the Humber, solid and shabby, waited on the cobbles.

" You been sold a pup," he said. " What you aiming to make of it, Harry boy—a furniture van, maybe?" He took the money, counted it slowly, and put it in his pocket.

" You're the new tenant," he said. He went through the front workshop and rolled up the door to the rear.

Harry Warrender inched the Humber in. Striker had the strip lighting on and the racks of tools on the walls gleamed; there was a pressure spraying machine, power-driven lathes, an electric welding plant—Striker reckoned that given forty-eight hours start he could remodel the coachwork of a car so that its owner wouldn't know it.

Harry began with some precise measurements in the back of the Humber; he took off his jacket and rolled up his sleeves and crawled underneath with a trailing light.

Striker went back to his office; he was doing some calculations that would have interested the Commissioners of Inland Revenue: Harry Warrender's cash contribution was but one of very many.

Later, when the pubs were open, Striker took his small van. He was back inside half an hour with bottled beer and some crab sandwiches.

Harry had the tailboard off the Humber and the flooring and he was saying rude things about rusted screws and broken bolts. He gave Striker ten shillings for the beer and sandwiches and said thanks there'd be no change and Striker could help himself to a beer.

He had made some rough sketches on the drawing board of what the Humber was going to have done to it. He chewed his sandwich very thoughtfully. On the wall in front of him there was a large coloured diagram of the oil and grease points of a popular family model, and in the middle of the diagram where the engine ought to have been somebody had pasted up a black-haired nude; Harry found himself wondering about Isabella Mundaya—so Charles had bumped into it after all.

Striker brought him back to reality. Striker didn't need any diagrams or engineering drawings as he indicated the way round the obvious snags. They discussed the job on the Humber in some detail, and for another fiver Striker undertook to ' find ' some materials.

Just before ten o'clock Harry cleaned himself up. He felt pleased with himself all round : progress had been made, tomorrow was Sunday and he could work all day uninterrupted, by Tuesday or Wednesday the paint and varnish would be dry and he could show Charles—and Isabella—the finished job.

Now it was Saturday night and he had a bit of money in his pocket and the promise of more to come.

Striker shut up shop and had a quick pint with him at the local. Harry collected a load of pennies and did some telephoning until he finally located Trudie.

Trudie was twenty-seven and getting to be just a little over the edge; at one time she had been a fairly popular fashion model until her involvement with the affairs of the night before made her less and less punctual for her ap-pointments, until in the end she had far more blank weeks than working hours; she had been married to a Naval officer but he had got tired of the gin parties that invariably finished with Trudie in somebody else's bed so he divorced her. Since then Trudie had been floating, but only just.

Harry liked her, not only for her considerable talent in the bedroom, but also because he felt she was a kindred spirit and both had known better days.

On the phone she was a little sulky at first because of his recent neglect; she was washing her hair and then going to bed.

Harry told her the last part was fine and just what he had in mind: he would bring both whisky and gin and be with her in twenty minutes.

Trudie agreed he had talked her round and she might spare him fifteen minutes.

Harry bave her a ribald comment which she loved entirely and went in search of a cab. Those lousy rooms at Kilburn wouldn't be seeing him at all that night.

Early the next morning he was back on the job and he worked right through the day, not even stopping for food; Striker brought him some more beer and a bag of ham rolls and gave him a hand when it came to matching up the heads of the screws and bolts that held the floor in place; they had used no new materials at any point. The false floor was in. No steel filings or patched paintwork or varnish or screw heads marked by screwdrivers—all old and shabby and scraped and uniform. The entrance to the false floor was under the tailboard, hidden by the number plate and the overhanging flap of the coachwork.

Striker crawled around the finished job. "Nice," he said. "Needs a spot more grease and some mud, Harry boy, and you've got yourself a snug little barrow."

" I think so," said Harry Warrender. " I'll leave it here
to dry off tomorrow. Pick it up on Tuesday. All right,
Striker? You just see those light-fingered louts of yours keep
away from it."

" Guard it with my life," said Striker. " Anybody likely
to come asking about it?"

Harry punched him in his elderly ribs and grinned.
" Striker, Striker, what a question. The legitimate owner
of that splendid vehicle knows I have it and approves of
what I have done with it."

" That makes a change," said Striker, " for both of us."

By the middle of the evening there was nothing more he
could do. They had tried out the Humber with Striker
squatting in the back listening for any rattles or rumbles
that oughtn't to be there. They brought the Humber back
and put it away. Harry bought Striker a drink at a pub in
Ladbrook Grove and wondered whether he could keep his
date with Trudie. He needed food and a night's sleep and
Trudie left him little time for sleeping. So he rang her up
and gave her some of the old charm : a bit of business had
come up and he couldn't get away.

Trudie laughed nastily and suggested the bit of business
wore a skirt. Harry told her how grievously she wronged
him : after last night did she really think he could look at
another woman? *Last night* : oh honey bunch—He gave
her more in the same vein and some details that the G.P.O.
would not have liked. They made a firm date for Tuesday.

Harry bought himself a good steak supper and went
back to Kilburn to sleep.

4

ON THE Monday afternoon Harry Warrender rang Charles Connell and reported on progress. He could produce the Humber for inspection by Wednesday at the latest.

Charles Connell was delighted. He had been in touch with Isabella and she had arranged to take her summer holidays at the end of the week. She'd go to Spain by air and be there waiting for them.

"Isabella thinks the camping idea is excellent," said Charles. "Just the right touch. The three of us ought to meet soon, Harry, and agree on the details. How about Wednesday? You bring the car to Weybridge—we could have dinner at the Anchor at Shepperton if we didn't fancy old Hopton's cooking. Isabella is very anxious to meet you."

"She'll never know how mutual it is," said Harry cheerfully. "Wednesday is a date. When do you plan for us to move off? Next week sometime?"

"Yes. Will that be all right with you?"

"I can make it," said Harry.

"I never really said thank you for coming in with me," said Charles. "I've thought about it a lot over the week-end, Harry—I took a lot for granted, I'm afraid."

"Let's not both be embarrassed," said Harry. "You're doing it out of chivalry and I need the money. I also

34

imagine Isabella must be quite a nice girl. I'm in a telephone booth at Piccadilly Circus and I'm sweating. I need
some beer."

Charles Connell in his bright new office behind Victoria
Street said nothing for a moment. Then, diffidently: " It
was all right about the Humber? I mean you had enough
money?"

" Plenty," said Harry, " but we may have to get a couple
of tyres: both the rear tyres are nearly bald and we'll be
carrying plenty of weight. I can pick up some at the right
price. Otherwise I'd say we're ready for the road."

" Get the tyres," said Charles. " Get anything you think
we ought to have—we don't want anything to go wrong
with the vehicle. I'll square up with you on Wednesday."

On Tuesday Harry Warrender collected the Humber
and arranged with Striker Lewis for a pair of good tyres;
there had been a steady summer rain all day and the roads
were greasy; he drove around Brentford and Hanwell and
as far out as Uxbridge, picking the dirtiest roads he could
find and making sure that the Humber got a liberal spatter-
ing of mud; in the space under the floor he had stuffed
kapok and sacking and even at speed the Humber made no
unusual noises.

In the evening he used the Humber to pick up Trudie
and take her out for several rounds of drinks and a little
food. She thought it was a hell of an old tank and suggested the mud was keeping it together. Harry demonstrated its paces and Trudie changed her mind : with some
nice cushions in the back she thought it had possibilities;
after a few more gins she wanted to climb into the back
and test her theory but Harry talked her out of it and took
her back to her flat, where they were both well content.

Charles Connell met Isabella outside her office just after six on Wednesday evening. In a brightly-figured summer dress of primrose and blue and white she looked crisp and fresh even after a heavy day's work answering the queries of harassed travellers in French and Spanish and English.

She was so exquisitely feminine and Charles Connell felt an obscure anger at himself for knowing that his old shyness and awkwardness hadn't altogether gone. It was always the same when he saw her coming towards him. He had never noticed before how much beauty and grace there could be in a woman's walk.

She had a narrow waist and small high breasts and it was impossible to think of her ever spreading into a heavy Spanish matron; her face was small and neat and faintly sun-tanned, with clear grey eyes and heavy tawny-blonde hair. When he looked at her and heard her voice and saw her smile he felt he had never known a woman before in all his life.

When she was with him, within reach of his hand, he was paralysed and beyond reasonable speech. Afterwards, when he thought about it, he could be brilliant and witty and uncompromisingly masterful.

They jockeyed into the home-streaming traffic. She kicked off her shoes, wriggled her small straight toes deliciously, and tucked them up under the spread hem of her skirt. " Do you mind, Charles?"

There were times when she seemed as boneless and pliable as a cat stretching itself.

" A rugged day?" he said.

" Brutal."

" We could swim, if we didn't have to meet Harry."

" Doesn't Harry swim?"

" It wouldn't be the same."

She was leaning back against the cushions, facing towards him.

" Charles, correct me if I'm wrong, but I've had the impression that you're not too anxious for me to meet Harry."

" He's all right. Up to a point, I mean."

" You made that sound terribly English. You went to the same school, you've known him for nearly twenty years —I don't remember meeting him at your home when we were children but you say I did so I must have. I'm curious about him."

" He'd be flattered if he knew. He cultivates women."

She laughed softly. " And you think that's a bad thing?"

He shot her a quick baffled look and said: " Harry makes a hobby of it. Chasing women—he always has done."

" He's not unique in that," she said demurely. " It's a fairly common pastime, I believe. Does Harry have much success?"

" I imagine so. Yes, I know damn well he does—he makes no secret about it."

" He sounds very ordinary."

" Perhaps. He'll probably make a pass at you before this is over."

She touched his sleeve, gently, smiling still. But it was a different kind of smile.

" And the idea of that upsets you, Charles. That's very sweet of you—I think I like that. But you really needn't worry: I've been earning my living since I was eighteen and I've had to handle men before, all sorts. It's sweet of you to be anxious on my account but I don't think it's necessary. We're using Harry Warrender because you know him and you think he's the right man for us—that's the only importance he can have."

"You're right," he said stiffly. "I'm afraid I must have sounded like an old auntie. I just didn't want there to be any unpleasantness for you. I know Harry. He thinks all women are fair game—I suppose the truth of the matter is that I've suddenly realised how jealous I could be."

"Of Harry Warrender? Oh, Charles!" Her laugh was clear and instant. Impulsively she slid her hand under his arm. At the sight of his unrelenting profile she said : " You don't know very much about women, do you ?"

"Less than nothing." He tried to make it sound light and flippant. "Perhaps it's time I started learning."

" I wonder."

He could feel the soft pressure of her hand and out of the tail of his eye he could tell she was watching. There was her fragrance—all the sweet fantasies of the past few weeks crowded in on him.

"You look terribly stern and full of purpose," she said softly.

He said it far more loudly than he had intended, the words just jumping out : " If there wasn't so much damned traffic I'd kiss you !"

He felt her hand withdrawing from his arm without haste. When he dared to look at her she was sitting with her hands folded in her lap. She was smiling as though she had just uncovered the wisdom of the ages.

" A little direct," she said, " but you're learning—I see you prefer the shock approach—"

" I meant it," he said. " I meant every word of it !"

" And so I should hope." She was smiling, sitting back in her corner.

He cleared his throat. There was a benighted fool in front of them with a large van, hogging the road and making no signals.

"Well," she said, "that clears that up. And if you apologise I'll scream and slap your face."

Under his urgent prodding the car achieved a special liveliness and they surged past the van with little to spare between them and on oncoming bus.

"For weeks," he told her, "for weeks I've been wanting to say something like that to you—long before you told me about your father and the paintings. I never thought I'd have the nerve."

"You make it sound a grim ordeal—ought I to be flattered? Most men don't *talk* much about kissing a girl, Charles."

He swung into the side of the road and stopped. He pulled her towards him and kissed her, not very expertly but quite wholeheartedly and without hurrying. The troublesome van rumbled past and the driver hooted derisively, or more probably enviously.

When he released her she said: "It wasn't so difficult after all, was it? Here, hold still." She took out her handkerchief and rubbed at his mouth, as though she had been doing it to him for years, and he found it a pleasantly intimate experience.

"Isabella," he said, "is this going to complicate things?"

She laughed, a warm low-pitched gurgle of a laugh. "Darling Charles, how you *worry*! I liked it—didn't you?"

"Yes, that's why—" He started driving again. "I wasn't just fooling around."

"Do you think I was?"

"No," he said fervently.

"Well then, that ought to be enough to be going on

with— we have a heavy business assignment in front of us."

Charles smiled, one of his rare smiles. " There's going to be plenty of time, later."

" I hope so," she said demurely.

The evening went well, Connell Senior had gone to a Conservative Club meeting, and Mrs. Hopton was happy to hear that the two visitors and Charles would be eating out.

Harry Warrender had the Humber ready for inspection. He wore one of his quieter suits and was altogether much less flamboyant than usual. With Isabella he was polite and correct and almost too obviously not over-interested. They drove across to the Anchor at Shepperton and had dinner by the window looking out on to the crowded car park with the church tucked into the corner and the rival hostelry opposite.

They discussed all aspects of the trip and Harry's intake of beer was surprisingly moderate in view of the circumstances. Later they went back to Weybridge and went over some maps and the two men listened to Isabella. She made a pretty thank-you speech to Harry without making too much of a business of it and something in her grey eyes warned Harry that this was going to be a business deal and nothing else.

He had been watching her all the evening in his own private fashion and he knew something had happened between her and Charles, something quite recent that had given Charles an uncharacteristic zip—he could imagine some interesting developments when they got to Spain.

Harry offered to drive Isabella back but Charles refused quite firmly on her behalf and without giving her the

option. That amused Harry. Before he left Charles got him
on his own and gave him an envelope and for the first
time in their long association Harry knew he was now the
employee.

He opened the envelope as soon as he was clear of the
house. The cheque was for three hundred pounds. He
wished he could go back to Charles and say: " Look, old
son, two hundred we agreed on—I don't need an extra
tip." He put the cheque back and drove on up to London.

The Kilburn rooms looked even lousier than usual. He
went across the landing for a bath. The landlady in the
basement didn't approve of baths after eleven o'clock at
night. It was nearly midnight and to hell with the landlady. He lay soaking and smoking. Isabella Mundaya—
now there was a body for you—Charles certainly wasn't
the boy to appreciate it.

When he came back from his bath he found he had a
visitor. Sandra. She had made herself comfortable on the
settee and she had found herself a drink. Her blonde hair
looked stringy and her skirt was too tight; she had her feet
up and she was showing most of her leg because she didn't
give a darn what she looked like when she was with him
any more than if she had been married to him for fifteen
years and the gloss had worn off.

" How the hell did you get in?" He lit a cigarette.

" You forgotten I got a key, duckie?"

" Then you can let yourself out. It's all over. Find
another mug."

" That's my sweet Harry-Boy talking." She laughed
huskily. " You can't ditch me as fast as that."

" It's all over," he repeated. " We agreed it was—what's
the sense, Sandra? I'm broke, you know I am—we'd only

fight—you wouldn't want to come back to a dump like this—"

She looked around the room. " It stinks all right," she said. " I never noticed it much before. Don't kid yourself, Harry, I'm not here to ask you to take me back. Personally I think you are a louse."

He grinned. Sandra never wrapped it up. " Well, you know I'll always be glad to see you, Sandra."

" Liar," she said. " I been hearing things about you, Harry. I hear you're in the money."

He shook his head, smiling. This was familiar ground between them. " I'm strapped. Sorry, my dear, but I can't do a thing—not at the moment."

" No? Then what's this? Tissue paper?" She opened her hand and showed him Charles Connell's cheque. " And I notice you've got your passport all ready in your pocket. You skipping out of the country, Harry?"

He took the cheque and stood over her. " One of these days I'll teach you to mind your own business."

She smiled. " This is my business." She tapped her stomach where the thin fabric of her skirt was stretched. " Your business as well, Harry, this time. I saw a doctor this morning. How would you fancy being a daddy?"

He sat down heavily, staring at her. " No," he said slowly, " it couldn't be—"

" I lived with you for five months," she said flatly. " There was nobody else, Harry, and you know it. I was crazy about you—is that funny? I'm going to need money and I'll take half that three hundred for a start—if you think you can nip out of the country and leave me to have your kid on my own you don't know your Sandra."

He punched his heavy thighs, scowling. " You mean you're going to have it?"

"That's my affair," she said, sitting up. "Don't offer to make an honest woman of me because I frankly can't stand the sight of you any more. I'll settle for the cash. I'll be around in the morning when the banks are open."

She stood up and yanked at her skirt and walked over to the door. A hippy strident near-blonde who knew how to look after herself. Almost.

"You messed me up, Harry. Now you got to pay for it. You better be here in the morning."

She banged the door behind her. Later he heard her quick steps on the pavement below his window. Sitting with the folded cheque in his hand he swore at the unfairness of it : Sandra would take him for every penny he had. He remembered the bitterness of their parting, and he remembered also her brother, that completely unpleasant young man with his Camden Town 'associates'—Tommy, who never held any recognisable job but always had money and was seldom alone; Harry had met him twice when things were just beginning between him and Sandra and Harry hadn't liked the silent contemptuous treatment Tommy had given him.

It was one thing to fiddle purchase tax and income tax and deal with the quick-cash boys in items of doubtful origin, it was quite another thing to find yourself brushing up against the mobs. Harry had seen some of their work and it didn't make him feel healthy.

Just before he got into bed he discovered Sandra had taken his passport. She'd be there in the morning with her hand out, and that was only the start.

He had lived with twelve or fifteen women for varying periods, he had never missed the chance of a quick pick-up —and it had to be lousy little Sandra who was going to fix him.

He sat up in bed with the last of his beer, scratching his hairy chest. This was going to be a good time to get out of London. As far as he knew he hadn't fathered a brat before, but the way he had been moving around you couldn't always be sure; it was something he had never worried about before. But if he knew Sandra, this was one time when he was going to do more than worry. He was going to pay.

5

SANDRA WAS on time in the morning. He was still asleep when she let herself in. She went into the bedroom. Harry wasn't a pleasant sight asleep with his mouth open.

She jabbed him in the side with the sharp corner of her handbag.

" Come on," she said. " We got a date."

He opened his eyes, grunted, and out of long habit reached out to pull her down.

She slapped his hand away. "You fat old goat, get up and dress yourself. I've come here for the money."

He watched her walk out into the living-room. She looked smarter than she had last night. Jaunty. Quite a swing of the hip.

When he went through to the bathroom she was behind the screen at the sink. Quite like old times, he thought, not that she had ever spent much time at the sink when they lived together.

He could talk her round. Offer her fifty and promise more—marry her? Well, he could talk about it and put on the old act, get her thinking about it. It was worth trying, it was *always* worth trying, in his experience.

When he was ready she had a cup of tea for him. But that was all. When he started to open negotiations she laughed at him with real contempt.

"You don't like to face it, do you, Harry? You got

nothing for me any more. You don't mean a damn thing. All I want from you is money. You were always a louse and you don't get any better."

Her thin face with the sharp chin was flushed. He tried another approach but she pushed his hand away angrily.

" Who's this Connell who gives you cheques for three hundred quid? What are you up to, Harry?"

" Business. A business deal. It isn't my money, Sandra— I might let you have fifty and then when things buck up a bit I'll see you right."

" Like hell you will." She sipped her tea. " Tommy says I ought to have the lot by rights, but I'll take half of it to be going on with." She smiled at him over her cup. " I don't think Tommy likes you very much either."

" I need my passport," he said heavily.

" We'll talk about that later," she said, standing up, smiling. " I'll keep it with me, Harry. It'll be okay and you can have it back when I decide—I wouldn't want you out of the country just now. See? You mightn't come back and I don't think I'd like that."

So they went to the bank and Harry cashed the cheque into fivers and saw half of them go into Sandra's bag, and what he was thinking showed in his face because Sandra said quite pleasantly :

" I wouldn't if I were you. Tommy and the boys would like the chance to carve you, Harry. I'll see you around and if I don't they'll come looking for you."

Harry Warrender went to the passport office and told them a circumstantial story about losing his passport. They were polite and sympathetic but he was reminded that the loss of a passport had to be followed by exhaustive enquiries. It was very unlikely that a new one could be issued to him in time for his proposed departure early next week.

So he'd have to get his own back from Sandra. To take her out and make her drunk wouldn't be difficult. Late in the afternoon he did a careful reconnaissance and found she had gone back to her old place over a dairy behind Mechlenburg Square. She wasn't working.

Sitting in the Humber that evening he watched her go out. She was hanging on to the arm of a young man in an Italian style suit with pronounced stripes; she was laughing and ready for fun; they got into a cream Prefect and drove off.

Harry waited ten minutes and then went round to the side door. The key was in the usual place on the ledge behind the dustbin. He let himself in and climbed up the narrow stairs.

The place was as he remembered it from when he first met her and before she moved in with him. Sandra was no housekeeper; there were her clothes everywhere, dirty glasses and cups and cigarette ends; the bed had been recently in use. He didn't find his passport. So she was carrying it around with her in her bag.

He rang Charles Connell at Weybridge and Charles wasn't terribly pleased to hear there might be a hitch over his passport; Isabella had booked her air passage for Sunday and they just had to be in Spain early in the week—

"All right, all right," said Harry. "I've just mislaid the ruddy thing—If I don't come across it I'll have to apply for a new one. You'll either have to wait or go without me."

"I'd wait, of course," said Charles Connell. "It would be damned inconvenient all round, Harry."

" I'm sorry. Maybe it'll turn up. Leave it to me. I'll keep in touch."

" Do," said Charles.

Just before midnight Harry Warrender returned to Sandra's place. The cream Prefect was outside and Sandra's light was on. He waited over half an hour. The light went out and the Prefect stayed where it was.

Harry gave it up. Sandra wasn't letting her condition interfere with her social life and she wasn't spending any time mourning for Harry Warrender.

He occupied himself on Friday with the Humber's working parts; his private feeling about engines stopped him from being satisfied with anything less than maximum efficiency, and the Humber had taken a heavy pounding in the past: Connell Senior had owned cars since the middle twenties without even learning much of what went on under the bonnet; a breakdown in the middle of this trip was something they could do without.

He rang Sandra three times on Saturday before he got her. She sounded as though she'd had a few drinks and she was at her short-lived mellow and amenable stage. To his surprise she agreed to meet him. All she said was that she hoped his chum Connell had been in touch with him because she could use the price of a new TV. set.

He said he thought it might be arranged. She was in good form when he picked her up an hour later. She had Harry where she wanted him and she wasn't going to let him forget.

They started on a pub-crawl, one of their old amusements: Sandra's exceptional capacity had been one of the things about her that had aroused his interest in the first

place. Harry carefully worked their itinerary westwards:
Sandra had made it plain she didn't intend to finish up in
bed with him at Kilburn; she didn't mind where the pubs
were as long as they sold liquor. All the time she kept a
tight hold on her bag. She was drunk but aware of what
was going on.

He bought a half-bottle of rum in one place. It was the
only drink that might put her under before she became
too screamingly impossible to handle.

He knew where he was going to take her and he was
beginning to feel the load of drink he'd taken himself.

The rum was making her sleepy. Good. They had left
the main road miles back. He found the side track with
the trees on either side. Sandra giggled as the Humber
bumped slowly along under the trees. There was a clearing at the end with the ruins of an old brick yard. He had
been there before, one summer afternoon with a young
Italian student-nurse. It was private enough for real sunbathing. Very private.

He switched off the lights. Sandra giggled again and
tried to sit up away from him. He pulled her towards him
and reached with his free hand for her bag.

" Hey," she said thickly, pushing at him:

It happened so quickly. It wasn't what he had been
planning to do. He hit her on the jaw. A quick savage
punch and he heard her teeth hit together. And her head
was limp against his arm.

" Sandra! Sandra—" Her head rolled as he moved her.
He smelt the sweetness of the rum and her perfume. He
touched her cheek, moist and soft. He whispered at her
fiercely, and when he took his arm away her whole body
rolled against the door.

He struck a match and held it in front of her face. Her

D

mouth was open now. And her eyes. And the flame of the match was steady by her mouth.

He got out and walked round the car in simple panic. Just one punch like that, almost accidental—it must have broken her neck, something like that.

He stayed out of the car for five or ten minutes, smoking, thinking, thinking—there was even a crazy hope that when he went back he'd find her all right. Just drunk.

In the end he got back in and sat in the dark, beside her. And it was quite a while before he could touch her. She was dead all right. No doubt about it now.

They'd never believe he hadn't meant to do it; too many people knew they'd been living together and that they'd had a hell of a fight and split up—and there was Tommy.

Harry Warrender wiped his hands very carefully on his handkerchief. He had got over his first attack of the shakes and he'd never felt so sober in his life. There was a chance this might be all right if he used his head.

He picked up the handbag that had started all the trouble. His passport was there. And four of the five-pound notes.

He got out and went round to the passenger's door. Sandra's body fell out against him as he opened the door and he couldn't make himself look at her face. He hoisted the body across his shoulders in a fireman's lift and picked his way over to the brick yard.

Behind one of the ruined outhouses there was an empty water tank with a wooden cover. He slid the cover back far enough and tipped the body over the edge. One of the shoes kicked him in the face as Sandra's legs slipped past him. He moved the cover back into place.

He ought to have taken her clothes, but that was more than he could face. He struck a match and found the fallen shoe. Back in the Humber he drank rum until his throat flamed and the shaking in his hands had stopped again. Before he left he found her other shoe and put in on the seat beside her bag.

Long before he reached Kilburn he was nearly himself again. It hadn't been his fault. She must have had a weakness somewhere. All he had intended was to get her drunk enough to let him get his passport—nobody would kill a woman over a thing like that—

He drove very carefully and soberly. He got rid of the shoe and the empty handbag, miles part from each other.

He slept very heavily: he had finished the rum when he got to bed. He spent Sunday morning, what was left of it, packing a couple of cases; the rent wasn't due for another two weeks and he was leaving no trace of himself behind. He wondered if Sandra's Tommy had known the Kilburn address.

He stood himself a good lunch and he had the feeling that even without what had happened to Sandra he would have made a clean break with the past. He'd been slipping fast; now that was over. He was blotting out last night completely from his mind.

Later in the afternoon he rang Charles at Weybridge and heard that Isabella had got away in the morning; he reported the recovery of his passport and Charles said that was fine. How about meeting for a drink in the evening.

"Charles," said Harry, "I've got the chance to sub-let my rooms to a chap and his wife. The point is they want to move in today. Could you put me up until we leave?"

"Of course," said Charles. "It couldn't be better, Harry. As a matter of fact I was going to suggest it—we

ought to spend some time on the final details before we
start. You come on down here as soon as you like."

Harry Warrender drove down to Weybridge in a much
easier frame of mind. He wasn't going to think of that
disused water tank in the ruined brickyard among the
trees. It couldn't have any connection with him now. In
two more days he'd be out of the country. It couldn't be
better.

PART TWO

"ARRIVING"

———————————

6

THERE WAS no trouble at all crossing into Spain at Irun. Harry Warrender was driving: like most good drivers he disliked being a passenger, and Continental roads, even when thick with June tourist traffic, were no bother to him.

They had maintained a high average all the way down through France; the Humber was loaded with gear: tents and sleeping-bags and cooking utensils—all of it second-hand. Their papers were in order, and they were so obviously just a pair of Englishmen on a cheap holiday with a heavy and inelegant vehicle.

The last leg was the one hundred and fifty miles along the coast road through San Sebastian and Bilbao to Santander which they reached late in the evening. Isabella Mundaya had booked rooms for them in a modest hotel behind the *Pereda* Gardens. There was a note from her for Charles and he passed it across to Harry: she would be coming in to meet them in the morning and she hoped they'd had a good trip; all was well at her end.

Harry folded the single sheet of paper. They were in Charles Connell's room waiting to go down to the late Spanish dinner and Harry was sitting on the edge of the bed. His face had caught the sun on the drive down; he looked heavy, almost flabby.

" Harry," said Charles, " I know this is a funny time to bring it up, but have you got any reservations about this trip?"

Harry Warrender looked at him briefly then stretched back on the bed, leaning on his elbows.

" What makes you ask that, Charles? We got here in good shape and faster than most people."

" I know. But you've got something on your mind, haven't you?"

" Who hasn't? Does it show all that much?"

" You've been quiet," said Charles.

Harry laughed. " I'm all right, Charles. Perhaps I needed this change of scene—I think London went a bit sour on me."

Charles watched him thoughtfully; ever since they had started he had imagined he was noticing a special tenseness and edginess in Harry and it didn't at all add up to what he had always thought Harry was.

" Put it out of your head," said Harry evenly, " whatever you're thinking, Charles. Nothing's wrong. From now on I promise to be the life and soul of the expedition— don't fuss about me, I'm not used to it."

Charles Connell picked his way carefully through dinner; most of what was offered his stomach would have trouble with, even the *gazpacho,* the ice-cold soup all visitors were expected to enthuse over; he made the most of his meal with delicate slices of *jamón servano,* pink mild mountain ham. Harry, on the other hand, worked his way through a handsome variety of dishes, and when he saw the price of a bottle of *Fundador* he abandoned his attempt to get on terms with the local beer: brandy as cheap as that ought not to be passed up.

Afterwards they walked in the cool of the breeze along the seafront on the *Paseo de Pereda* towards the docks and the old fishing quarter; there were yachts and cruisers of all sizes squatting in the dark waters of the bay, and the promenade was crowded with strollers; there seemed to be a surprisingly high proportion of young children, bright-eyed and voluble even though it was after eleven o'clock.

When they got back to the hotel Harry said he felt like looking around further, especially since they'd be moving out to assume their role as campers the next day.

" I like the look of this place," he said lazily.

Since it was clear he didn't want any company Charles went in and up to bed. He could imagine the sequence of events : it wouldn't take Harry long to find the most promising night spot in the place; in the hall of their hotel, among the notices of local attractions, there had been details of entertainments ' suitable for the family ', and as he went up to his room Charles was quite certain that Harry would find what he wanted; officially night clubs were supposed to close at one o'clock, but outside the town limits there were few restrictions.

They had had one short night in Paris on the way down and Harry had been remarkably circumspect; dinner, a modest couple of drinks, and then bed; in fact it had really been Harry's moderation in Paris that had convinced Charles something was wrong—Harry Warrender in Paris with some money in his pocket for just the one night ought to have meant something more than an early bed-time—and it hadn't been the four hundred and seventy mile trip to the Spanish frontier that had bothered Harry : driving was no chore to him. He had been unusually subdued and very short on conversation so much so that Charles Connell had begun to think that he might be regretting the trip—

not in itself a very good omen since Charles knew he was going to be relying on Harry all the way through.

And then there had been Harry's anxiety to get hold of an English newspaper before they left Paris, and he had gone to considerable trouble about it—which hadn't really been like Harry who seldom bothered with anything more than the boldest headlines at home—and pictures of any young women who were attracting attention. So it was really a relief to have Harry acting in character again. It was three o'clock when noises in the next room woke Charles briefly. Harry was back and perhaps just a little drunk to judge by the long intervals between the thumps of his shoes on the floor. Santander had apparently lived up to his expectation.

Isabella arrived on the country bus in the middle of the morning; she looked very summery in a dark blue skirt and a white blouse that stressed her soft even suntan, and she carried a yellow wide-brimmed straw hat.

Tactfully Harry Warrender busied himself with the Humber; Isabella looked even better he thought than when he had seen her last and she knew damn well what he'd been thinking when their eyes met; Harry could never see any reason for not letting a woman know when he admired her : so he had got the message across and she could make of it what she liked; the faint flush under her tan and the way her eyes had shifted told him that he was registering.

It might be amusing to cut Charles out, because Charles was so obviously yammering over the girl, and she was encouraging him quite nicely—the little flutter of her fingers on his arm as she spoke to him and the slow smile up into his face, almost pretending Harry Warrender wasn't there,

They had coffee at an open air café before leaving. Isabella took Charles's arm and Charles was visibly delighted and inches taller. Harry Warrender watched the swing of her hips: she was so pointedly ignoring him except for the merest scrapings of politeness. He was just the driver. To mark his independence he skipped the coffee and ordered a large *Andaluza,* a mixture of dry sherry, orange juice and soda water with a large chunk of ice; he gave his attention to a couple of American women at a nearby table: mother and young daughter and the mother was much the more interesting—a good figure and some excellent jewellery. Reluctantly Harry let himself be drawn back to their immediate plans.

Before they left there was some shopping to be done, according to Isabella, mostly tinned foods; their pose as touring campers was going to be a reality, it seemed, but she promised it wouldn't be too rugged, and at least the weather would be on their side.

They drove into the country beyond Solares; they ran through a succession of steep valleys, thickly wooded and cool. Isabella was giving the directions and they were climbing all the time, now on country roads with poor surfaces and some bewildering bends. There were small orchards with bright blossoms and small whitewashed farmhouses stuck to the sides of the hills; sleek dairy herds in lush meadows under the shadow of the dark trees.

Later the gradients increased and the vegetation was thinner; outcrops of grey rock broke the sides of the hills and the grass looked coarse and scrubby. In front of them were the shadowy outlines of the *Picos de Europa.*

They topped a ridge fringed with pines and followed the winding road down; a slender stream flashed in the sun

and darted under an old narrow bridge just wide enough
to let the Humber through.

Some miles later when they had come down to where
the valley flattened out and the trees began again Isabella
said :

" You take the path on the left, up into the field."

There were some off-white goats and a dusty grey donkey,
a pond under some trees and some tired thin cattle standing in the shade swinging their tails at the flies. Beyond the
trees there were old farm buildings, mostly single storey with
long untidy roofs. A dog barked at their approach and
a young man appeared round the corner of one of the buildings wiping his hands on the seat of his patched trousers;
he wore a faded blue shirt, collar-less and open at the
neck; he was very brown with thick black hair, matted
with sweat, and the dark sweat patches under his arm-pits
spread out to his chest. He looked tough and cheerful.

" Here's Guillermo," Isabella said softly. " It's his father's
farm but Guillermo works it since his father became bed-
ridden—he speaks English. He used to work in a hotel
in London—all the land round here was once part of the
Mundaya estates. The place where my father is staying is
about two miles away. You'll have to camp here—it's all
arranged. It won't be for long and Guillermo will let you
have eggs and milk; there's only one bedroom at the farm
and you wouldn't find it very comfortable—elderly Spanish
countrymen don't like fresh air inside their houses—"

Guillermo had reached the Humber. His heavy face
broke into a grin and he held up a large hand :

" *Salud* ! Welcome !"

Isabella introduced them and Guillermo's handshake was
proudly muscular. Any friends of the Señorita's were his to
command. He had picked out the very spot for them to

camp and he assured them that his house was their house for as long as the gentlemen pleased. Guillermo's country odour was strong but his goodwill was unmistakable.

They backed the Humber up under some trees, some fifty yards from the farm buildings, and started to unpack in the shade. A small barefooted boy arrived. He was a miniature Guillermo and at first he was shyly formal and polite.

"This is Chico," said Isabella, "going to be a great *torero* one day, or else a bishop. He hasn't quite decided which."

Chico smiled and jerked his thin shoulders. Later he thawed and helped them to put up the two small tents in the lee of the Humber; the collapsible canvas washbasin-cum-bath excited his profoundest admiration since he clearly could not understand anyone going to all that trouble merely for the sake of washing, a duty that Chico avoided whenever possible; no doubt it was different if one had the misfortune to be born *inglés*.

Eventually Guillermo hauled his son back to the sun-drenched silence of the farm. Charles Connell stretched out in the shade; it was almost too hot to smoke.

"This is no hardship," he said. "We've got everything we need—so long as we're posing as open-air hearties we might as well make it authentic."

"Nice of you to take it like that." Isabella was sitting on a blanket with her blue skirt spread about her. "I had hoped to get you proper accommodation, but you can see how far off the map we are—but at least it's fine. If you stopped in the village down the hill there'd be too much gossip: what you were doing and how long you were stay-ing—it would get round to the *Guardia Civil* and we don't want them showing any interest."

" We certainly don't," said Charles.

Harry Warrender lay on his stomach with his head pillowed on his arms, apparently sleeping. He had been quiet for some time. He stirred and turned his head to look at Isabella.

" When do we go into action?"

" Tomorrow night, we hope."

" And how many of the locals know about it? This fellow, Guillermo for instance—does he know what it's all about? Does he really think we're just a couple of innocent campers?"

" All Guillermo needs to know is that you are friends of mine." Isabella's voice was stiff.

Harry grinned. He knew Charles was looking at him without favour. To hell with Charles.

" Why don't we operate tonight then?" he said. " We're here."

" We discussed all that this morning," said Charles flatly, " at Santander, Harry—I don't think you can have been listening."

" Sorry teacher—I must have been admiring the adjacent scenery."

Nobody smiled. Harry sat slowly up and dusted the grass from his hands.

" Carceros and his wife left yesterday," Isabella said. " They are going to San Sebastian first and then across to Barcelona—he has business interests there. The servants are still in the house but most of them will be gone by tomorrow : that will be the time for us to go there, surely— at least, that is my father's view and I agree with him. It would be silly to take any needless risks at this stage."

She looked across at Charles and he nodded.

" I don't see any desperate hurry now," he said. " We

have to go actually into the house to reach the pictures, don't we?"

"Yes. It wouldn't be at all safe with the place full of servants and the family in residence—Carceres likes to live in style." She couldn't keep the note of bitterness out of her voice. "For a country villa it's rather spacious—some of it very old; my grandfather added new wings and servants' quarters and extra stables—he was a great horseman in his day; captained the Spanish team all over the world at one time. My father would like to meet you both this evening—he's terribly grateful for what you are doing. If we get the pictures— "

—"No if about it," said Charles Connell. "Am I right, Harry?"

Harry Warrender nodded, looking at the girl.

"How many servants will be left in the house?" he asked.

"Three or four, and when Carceres is away they help themselves to his wine—we hope they will be drunk. That should make it easier." Although she was answering his question she was looking at Charles.

Harry smiled. He had needled her and that was sometimes not a bad way to start: at least it meant they were aware of you.

"Your information about the house is reliable, I suppose?" Harry took out his cigarettes.

"It is," she said shortly. "The Mundayas used to be important people around here."

"You make me feel like a peasant," said Harry lightly, lighting a cigarette.

Charles Connell noted the colour in Isabella's face, the tiny tightening of her mouth and nostrils. Harry was being clumsily offensive, and that wasn't like him.

Charles stood up and held out his hand: " It's nearly two o'clock—I think an intake of food is indicated."

In one lithe uncoiling movement Isabella stood beside him. Harry closed his eyes and pretended to sleep. Let them hold hands and get lunch.

In the middle of their picnic meal Chico arrived with a large earthenware jug of coffee and a home-made basket of fruit; with very little urging he joined them after agreeing that he had already eaten at home : one could eat at home any day and there was never enough when one had the appetite of a man; furthermore the idea of food from tins fascinated him, and Charles Connell produced a bottle of *Mondariz,* the fizzy mineral water that represented champagne in Chico's vocabulary.

Squatting cross-legged beside Isabella he announced that he found Charles Connell *muy simpatico.* It had the makings of a pleasant party until Guillermo appeared at the open door of a low barn and shouted; Chico collected the empty coffee jug and basket, said a grave *adios* all round, and went to do papa's bidding.

Harry Warrender slipped off his shoes, rolled a blanket under his head and went noisily to sleep. Isabella said she ought to be going back; she'd go by the fields and over the hill; she insisted it wasn't worth taking the car.

Charles walked with her. They skirted the rear of Guillermo's small farm and found shade in a small wood that marched quietly up the side of the hill.

" I don't like him," she said. " The more I see of him, Charles, the less I like him—I'd feel much happier if he hadn't come—he makes me uneasy—there's something about him that's all wrong, I think—and I don't quite know what it is. It's not only the way he looks at me—"

Charles took her arm. " It won't be for much longer.

And I think I know exactly what you mean—but you won't have to see much more of him, not after tomorrow."

She wrinkled her nose smiling. " And the absurd part of it is that we really do have to be grateful to him for what he did to the car—my father was most interested when I told him. It will be all right, won't it, Charles?"

" I'm sure of it," he said.

" You're both invited to dinner with us tonight. Don't expect anything very grand, will you—father wants to talk about the house and tomorrow night and he wants to see the car for himself."

They didn't hurry. Charles told her what a hell of a long time it had been since he had seen her off on the plane at London Airport on Sunday morning, and they found themselves in pleasant agreement over a number of things quite unconnected with paintings by Zurbaran.

E

7

It was dark when they went to see Luis Mundaya and Guillermo rode with them to show them the way; he had business in that direction, he said. After a mile of country road they were on rough tracks that needed all of the Humber's ground clearance and general stability. It was real country motoring.

Harry Warrender said very little except for an occasional muttered expletive at some of the deep dried ruts. He had been still sleeping when Charles had returned after seeing Isabella back.

When night came Guillermo had arrived in a clean white shirt, with an oil lamp; the three of them had sat round it, smoking; Harry Warrender and Guillermo had shared the bottle of *Fundador* Harry had bought in Santander. It had been an awkward and artificial interlude and Charles Connell had been glad when it was time for them to be moving on; Harry had sunk back into his odd former uncommunicative mood as though he really didn't give a damn what happened; the brandy made him sweat but he said he had to drink something, for God's sake.

The farm where Luis Mundaya was staying was rather larger than Guillermo's and in a better state of repair. The Humber's lights showed up barns and cowsheds and a solid farmhouse. A dog at the back rattled its chain and barked ferociously and madly at their approach.

66

Guillermo wished them a pleasant evening and went off back down the track. He had put on a dark jersey and was soon invisible.

Isabella met them at the door. With the soft lamplight behind her she was extraordinarily beautiful and graceful, and Charles Connell thought that the special quick smile she gave him was the most exhilarating thing he had ever seen.

She lifted her hand to the enveloping darkness beyond the lights of the car. "You'd never have found it on your own, would you? It really *is* a country retreat—come and meet my father."

The living-room was low and dark and smelt of age and generations of past living; the floor was stone with coloured rush mats and a dark rug in front of the wide fireplace scooped out of the wall and deep enough for most of the family to sit round three sides of it on a winter's night.

Luis Mundaya got up from a straight-backed chair when they came in.

It was some twenty-five years since Charles Connell had seen him; the Luis Mundaya he could vaguely remember had been an elegant quick-moving man with a ready infectious laugh and an exotic cream Delage touring car, visiting their sedate Weybridge house and sweeping his father and mother up to London for dinners and theatres and supper parties; very much a magical visitor from another and a more glittering world; for years afterwards the aroma of a cigar had reminded Charles of Luis Mundaya and his father sitting on their small veranda and talking of their Cambridge days together, while the river floated gently past.

This was a very different Luis Mundaya: a thin triangular face with the skin stretched tightly over the bones, deep sunken eyes, his hair white and still abundant, he held his left arm tightly across his chest, the thin shoulder thrusting awkwardly forward and hunched. He looked so thin and wispy and tired. Charles Connell thought of the brown muscular man who used to beat his father so soundly at tennis and then swim to the furthest bend of the Wey and back without bothering.

"Hullo, Charles," said Luis Mundaya in a casual voice. "It's been quite a while. How is your father?"

"Very well, thank you. He sends his respects—may I introduce Harry Warrender, a friend of mine—"

"Delighted," said Luis Mundaya. "I understand you have been very clever over the car, Mr. Warrender. I am indeed grateful to you and I shall be most interested to see what you have contrived. My daughter is most enthusiastic about the idea. Quite ingenious, she tells me."

Harry Warrender rubbed his nose and grinned. "I'm not claiming any patent, sir. It's been done before—we'll just have to hope that our luck holds."

"We will indeed. But I think a sherry before we talk business? Isabella, my dear, I really think the *fino* is the only drink for this occasion. We entertain seldom, gentlemen, as you can well imagine, and I would value your opinion of this wine. Charles, my dear boy, I hear good things of you. Splendid, splendid. And your father has taken up golf at last—he always swore he never would!"

"He's enthusiastic and erratic." Charles Connell smiled. "But it keeps him healthy. He often talks of you—he would have liked to come on this trip with us."

"You must get him to come to Santander. Soon. I would like to see him again, Charles—and he could practise his golf: the *Pedreña* course is the finest in Spain, I believe." Luis Mundaya was smiling politely as though all this could ever be a reality. " Later, Charles, we will talk of this and you must tell me of your work : it is a great and satisfying thing to be one of those who build because building is for the future and too many of us spend our lives pulling things down—"

Isabella came in with the sherry and some glasses. The sherry was dry and clean and full of sunshine. As he drank Charles Connell met Isabella's level gaze and his toast was a private one and he found himself praying that she would share it.

Later they took a lamp and went out to the Humber and Harry demonstrated his handiwork.

Luis Mundaya shook his head in wonderment.

" I am no mechanic, Mr. Warrender, but I must confess that I would never have suspected what you have done. It is quite admirable."

" It'll pass," said Harry, " or we're all in for a lot of trouble." He was smiling but something in the tone of his voice didn't fit the expression on his face.

" I take it you are a man of experience, Mr. Warrender," said Mundaya softly. " I would be interested to hear that you have no misgivings about what you are doing." Charles and Isabella had gone back into the house.

" I am concerned only with pulling it off," said Harry and was glad that it was dark; there was an uncomfortably penetrating quality about the old man's gaze; it wasn't impossible to imagine him as a difficult and unco-operative prisoner, yielding nothing ever of his own principles.

Before they went back into the house Luis Mundaya touched Harry Warrender's sleeve very lightly, in the fashion of a man who offers a friendly warning : " I have always admired the English idea of fair play, Mr. Warrender—it suggests some important values and an adult sense of proportion. I also remember an American expression about never giving a sucker an even break—"

Harry Warrender lit a cigarette, hoping mainly to see the old man's face in the flare of his match, but Mundaya had turned away and was looking out over the dark countryside, his white hair a faint blur above his face. Mundaya was tottery and battered and looked at the end of his tether, but he still wasn't a good man to fool with; all that Harry Warrender had heard about him from Charles was now quite credible.

" Mr. Warrender," said Mundaya and there was now no pretence at all of urbanity in his voice; it was the voice of a man who had given orders in his time and exacted obedience, " my daughter imagines we are selling the pictures so that the money can come to me here in my country." He had moved closer and his voice was low : " I need very little now and I have very little time. I want the money to go to her—if things had been otherwise she would have been a considerable heiress. I have a letter for Joachim Menendez with my wishes—Isabella would be angry if she knew. Mr. Warrender, I am already in your debt : will you deliver the letter for me ? It will only be important if and when the paintings reach Menendez, so I do not wish to use the post."

" All right," said Harry Warrender, " but why didn't you ask Charles ? I'm the only stranger here."

" I doubt if Charles could keep anything important from Isabella. They are in love, I think, and he is not a subtle young man—I fear he would give himself away before it was time and Isabella would be upset. I am anxious myself for only one thing, Mr. Warrender : I want my daughter to have the money—Joachim Menendez will do as I ask."

He gave Warrender a thick square envelope. Harry Warrender slipped it into his pocket.

" What happens when Isabella finds out what you've done? Suppose she refuses to use the money?"

" It will be too late." Luis Mundaya turned to the open door of the house behind them. " There is an excellent young doctor at Molledo, Mr. Warrender, and he has been very honest with me. The coming winter will be my last. I will have no need for money. Shall we go in to dinner?"

Throughout the meal that followed Harry Warrender wondered at the old man's composure. Sitting at the head of the scrubbed oak table in the lamplight he invested the plain country fare with the dignity of a banquet; living in obscurity now, and after all those years in Spanish jails, stripped of his property and knowing that his span was ending, he was still able to make Harry Warrender feel that he was looking at a man of real quality. It was easy to see why his daughter treasured him.

When they got round to their plans for the next night Luis Mundaya announced that he intended to go with Charles and Harry and they found it impossible to argue him out of it.

" I put the paintings where they are : I will be there to get them out," he said pleasantly and firmly. " The police searched the house and grounds in vain. They brought in special men from Madrid. Alleged experts. And they went back empty-handed. Perhaps also I have a wish to see my own house once more—my wife and I were happy there so many years ago."

He smiled round at the other three. " Am I being whimsical? Or do you feel that I am so crippled I will handicap you? I think I can find the strength." He reached across the table and patted Isabella's hand briefly. "For one night I am coming out of my retreat and it will be in a good cause. I can show our two friends here a way into the house that defeated one of the best policemen Franco ever had. You must indulge me in this, my dear. I am insisting."

"Father," said Isabella, and then shook her head.

"That's better," he said gently. "You know it is no use arguing with me these days, and you are not going to come with us. You will wait here until we return. Please, my dear, that is what I wish."

Isabella looked at Charles and shrugged: "And I suppose you'll agree with that, Charles?"

"Frankly," he said, "I do. Not that we expect anything to go wrong—but I'm sure Harry and I will feel easier if we know you're all right—"

Isabella smiled in a way that made Charles feel he was the only other person in the room.

"The logic of that escapes me," she said, "but I can see I'm out-voted. I'll be the patient little woman with the coffee and brandy all ready."

"Brandy," said Luis Mundaya, "now that reminds me. My dear patient Isabella, we are neglecting our guests. These empty glasses insult our Mundaya honour. Are we now so lost to civilised custom that guests at our table must remain thirsty?"

Isabella bent and kissed the top of his head as she passed.

"Well at least they're sober," she said placidly.

Luis Mundaya placed his thin bony hands on the rough unpolished surface of the table, and his left arm he could move only with extreme difficulty. His shadow on the wall behind him from the lamp was grotesque: all head and sloping shoulders,

"This is a strange business we have been preparing," he said. "Plotting like bandits—planning like thieves in the night."

Charles Connell cleared his throat. "It seemed like a pretty sound idea to me," he said, "as soon as I heard about it from Isabella. After all, sir, the paintings are yours. I don't look upon it as wrong at all, and neither does Harry. Isn't that right, Harry?"

"Of course," said Harry Warrender. "I think Mr. Mundaya knows what we think. We're here."

Luis Mundaya stroked the edge of the table with the fingers of his right hand, and Charles noticed for the first time that he had lost the first joints of all four fingers on his left hand.

"Charles," said Luis Mundaya, "what did your father think of this?"

"Well," said Charles carefully. "It's difficult to say."

"You told him?"

"Not altogether. Not the actual details."

"So if the next things he hears of you is that you are in prison in Spain he will not know what it is all about?"

"He knows we're on a bit of a special trip," said Charles doggedly, "and he knows we're going to be seeing you." He smiled. "I imagine he knows there's something irregular about it, but he didn't ask and I didn't tell him."

"I ought to send you away," said Luis Mundaya slowly. "I owe it to your father."

"I wouldn't go. Not now."

Charles sat with his elbows on the table so that his face was in the pool of light from the lamp, and watching him Harry Warrender thought he had never seen Charles look so determined. Almost tough. It was surprising. Isabella stood behind him, her hands resting on the back of his chair, serious, unmoving.

" It's no good discussing it any further, sir," said Charles. " If he knew, my father wouldn't have me behave any differently. And if you don't believe that you must have forgotten about him."

Luis Mundaya smiled, gently, his thin ravaged face softening. He lowered his head.

" I deserved that, Charles. I am lucky in my friends, especially at a time like this." He looked at Harry Warrender and said : " I hope I may now include you in that number, Mr. Warrender."

" I hope so," said Harry Warrender politely. " I feel I have an interest in this affair—more than ever now that we have met."

Luis Mundaya nodded. Isabella brought the cognac, and cigars. It was normal again.

Later Charles Connell lay in his tent; it was quiet and unfamiliar and he was having trouble sleeping; the sleeping-bag was padded and Guillermo had given them some clean straw, but the ground was still uncompromisingly hard and unrelaxing even after the day they had had.

It was two o'clock and he was in a broken unsatisfactory doze when he heard Harry moving in the next tent; Harry had boasted that he could sleep anywhere.

Charles waited, wide awake now. Harry was standing outside his tent in the dark, listening. It was unlike Harry to be so considerate. Charles got himself up on one elbow, he was about to call out and ask what was wrong. Then he heard the soft slide of Harry's feet over the grass, going away. And presently a faint clinking metallic noise from where the car was parked.

Carefully he worked his way to the flap beyond his head and lifted one corner.

Harry had a torch. He was under the tail of the Humber on his hands and knees doing something to the false bottom. It was an odd hour for him to be satisfying himself that his work was still all right.

He was removing some of the packing. He took something out, played the beam of his torch over it, and rubbed it on the denim trousers he wore in place of pyjamas. Then he put all the packing back. When he crawled out from under the Humber he went round and opened the driver's door.

Charles wriggled back into his tent. It would have been easy to go across then and there and challenge Harry. Charles lay on his back, staring at the dim white spread of the tent. He heard Harry return and settle down. They had discussed the point before they left Weybridge and they had been in agreement. So why had Harry brought a gun?

If Harry felt they were going to need a gun, in spite of the fact that they had agreed it wouldn't be a good thing to bring one, it suggested a disturbing lack of mutual trust. And that was surely no way to start on the difficult thing they were going to do tomorrow night. It needed thinking over.

Charles was asleep before he came to any satisfactory conclusion.

8

THE NEXT morning Charles waited for a chance to examine the Humber and locate the gun. Whatever Harry had in his mind he was keeping to himself; stripped to the waist he had stood in the bright morning sun and noisily washed himself in the stingingly cold stream water brought over by Guillermo with some milk and eggs; Chico had been sent mutinously off to attend the village school, but not before he had milked the goats and helped his father with the cows: the life of a small boy on a tiny Spanish farm was clearly no sinecure, not with a papa like Guillermo.

Harry asked Guillermo about petrol and found he had seven or eight miles to drive. At Luis Mundaya's house the night before they had decided that as soon as the Zurbarans were stowed away Charles and Harry would pick up their gear and start on the return to Irun. So that meant the Humber was going to need all the petrol it could hold: there could be no easing up at least until they were across the frontier.

"You coming, Charles?" Harry picked up his jacket.

"No," said Charles.

Harry smiled. "Expecting Isabella?"

"Yes."

"Then you won't need me."

"No."

"Straight from the shoulder. You know, Charles, I don't think she likes me."

Charles said nothing. They were walking over to the Humber. Harry lit a cigarette and spun the match into the air with a flick of his thumb.

"I wonder why, Charles? Am I so hard to take?"

"Does it matter?"

Harry lifted one shoulder. "As a matter of cold sober fact, no."

"Then it's really all right, isn't it?" said Charles pleasantly.

Harry looked at him thoughtfully for a moment and it was on the tip of Charles's tongue to ask it: "Why the gun, Harry?" Instead he said: "You seemed to be getting on all right with old Luis last night."

"That's right, I did." Harry climbed into the Humber and pressed the starter. "See you soon."

Charles watched the car bump down the track and he felt more uneasy than he could explain to himself. He tidied up their small camp in what he could remember of the Boy Scout fashion, and started up over the hill to the wood to meet Isabella; at the back door of Guillermo's farm a young woman in an apron watched him with a baby on her arm; when he waved she lifted one hand hesitantly, and then quickly went back in; from the shape of her there was another addition to the family well on the way.

Isabella reported that her father was out walking somewhere under the trees.

"He's restless," she said, "and he can't bear to be inside —I suppose that's the effect of prison. Every day he walks; if he has to spend a day inside he can't sleep. How did you think he looked last night?"

"Very spry," said Charles. "He surprised me—I wish we could persuade him to come to England."

"He would never agree. I've talked to him and talked to him, but it isn't any use. I wanted to stay here with him, get a more comfortable place and look after him." She smiled. "He wouldn't hear of it."

"I agree with him there," said Charles steadily, "and you know why. I want you in England with me. I love you."

"I know," said Isabella softly. "And I love you, Charles—"

Eulalia, the housekeeper, came in with coffee and pastries; she was a large dark square woman with a high undivided bosom like a shelf; a widow for many years, she was deaf and eternally smiling and she spoke no English; in her scheme of things the Señor Luis Mundaya ranked a little below the Holy Father in Rome perhaps.

She stood over them, smiling, with her large arms folded and it was impossible to avoid the pastries.

"We've just plighted our troth," said Charles. "I never thought it would be over cream puffs with raisins on top. Tell her the grub is wonderful, darling, and perhaps she'll beat it back to the kitchen. She's crowding me."

Isabella retailed the compliment in loud emphatic Spanish. Eulalia bowed to him with considerable dignity, and *artiste* acknowledging the merited recognition of her genius. She said something to Charles that had Isabella smiling, and then she steamed out of the room.

"What was all that?" said Charles. "The last bit? You're looking girlish."

"She said you would be the father of strong sons, but you must eat more: you made a very poor dinner last night, she says, and that worries her."

"I see," said Charles. "Well, skipping the diet advice what do you feel about the first proposition?"

"I am covered in confusion," said Isabella, "naturally."

"I'll have to tell your father. Soon."

"He knows," she said. "He knew as soon as I arrived here—you don't imagine I could keep a thing like that from him, do you? He's very happy about it: I think he had a sneaking fear that I'd marry some quite unsuitable Englishman but now he know it's all right. And I'm happy."

She sat with the sunlight slanting across her, smiling, poised, very lovely in every way; the sunlight softened and warmed the rich tawny tints in her hair.

"I wish I could paint you, just like that," said Charles. "Maybe that's not a terribly original ambition and I can't paint for peanuts. I only feel really alive when I'm with you. You make me know everything I've been missing—it's like opening a door and outside you find everything you've ever wanted. Am I making any sense? I'm thirty-five with a lousy digestion and I'm the dullest company I know. But when you're around I don't think there's anything I couldn't do. Is that sense?"

"The best," she said softly. "And don't ever let it be any different."

He went over to her and drew her up towards him with a solemn seriousness until all of her was against him. He was so grave, purposeful.

"We're going to get married soon," he told her and as her supple waist yielded in to him he repeated fiercely against her neck: "Soon, my darling, oh soon!"

And the force of her answering arms and seeking mouth held them together in long unmoving moments while the sunlight played around them; and when they drew apart she still hung in the curve of his arm with her eyes drowsily half-closed, murmuring:

"It must be very soon, Charles, darling—please—"

They walked out into the sun, to look for Luis; until they reached the shade of the trees the heat was savage and merciless, and Isabella said she was sure her father would be resting somewhere in the cool.

They didn't find him. Instead they met José on his bicycle, sweating his way up the track towards the house.

José was a powerfully built man, rather older than Charles, just beginning to run to fat; it was in his farmhouse that Luis Mundaya was living; José's grey shirt was plastered to his muscular chest, his blue linen trousers had been washed and washed until they were nearly as faded grey as his shirt.

His bicycle was an old high-framed model with one brake only and a string saddle. José let it slither away from him when he saw Isabella; he left it on the track with its rusty wheels spinning as he came over to them, wiping his streaming face on the sleeve of his shirt.

The conversation that followed was energetic and full of drama and sweeping gesticulations from José. "*Señora Carceres*" were the only two words that Charles understood from all the eloquence, but from the expression on Isabella's face she wasn't hearing good news.

Charles offered José a cigarette and Isabella explained: José had been across to the other side of the valley and he had seen Señora Ludmilla Carceres returning to the house in her white *automóvil*; she hadn't been alone and the man with her wasn't Señor Carceres. José had seen the man carrying suitcases into the house.

"Damn," said Isabella. "She's supposed to be on the

way to Barcelona with her husband. This complicates things—the cases suggest she's staying. Oh damn and damn, why did she have to pick now to bring a boy friend home?"

" It's like that, is it?" said Charles.

" Yes, very much so. She's twenty years younger than her husband. She's known round here as the French tart— I believe Carceres met her when she was dancing at Nice. Normally she's a little more discreet than this."

José squatted in the shade, his strong hands dangling between his thighs; he said something about Señora Carceres that was certainly unflattering and spat to emphasise his point.

" Does José know what we're up to?" said Charles softly.

" He's been watching the house for us. I don't know what he may have guessed, but he's perfectly safe. Carceres is now his landlord and a very bad one—José's father and grandfather and great-grandfather were Mundaya tenants, and to José my father is still the *patrón*. Whatever the Mundayas do is likely to be all right with José. He's going over there again this afternoon to see what he can find out."

" I'll go with him," said Charles. " This isn't going to spoil tonight; we won't let it, even if the lady and her admirer are temporarily in residence."

Isabella talked to José and José nodded and smiled at Charles: he was with the Señorita and that made him all right with José.

On the way back they met Chico returning from his reluctant schooling. He had a message: the Señor Luis was with Padre Bartolomeo and would not be returning until after *siesta*.

" They play chess together and talk," said Isabella, " mostly they argue. The Padre is the only one who visits

F

my father still. I suppose we'd better have Harry over for lunch—we can't leave him on his own."

" I wish we could," said Charles, " but it wouldn't do. He was asking me this morning why you didn't like him."

Isabella laughed softly. " I'll get Chico to take a message to him and I'll be the charming hostess when he arrives. I wouldn't want to damage his self esteem. What did you tell him, darling? That I thought he was a gross vulgar fat man? That I just couldn't *bear* having him near me?"

" Not exactly. I slid round it with my customary finesse and we sort of let it drop."

Harry drove up twenty minutes later and parked the Humber in the shade. The tank was full and he had bought some extra cans as well; he had done some local driving around, including the neighbourhood of their objective.

Charles told him about the unwelcome and unexpected return of Señora Carceres and at first Harry had found it funny.

" A lady of enterprise," he said.

" A slut," said Isabella sweetly. " The house was once my home. I was born there, so you must excuse me if I can't share your enthusiasm."

Harry grinned, undefeated, and went back to his grilled trout.

" The point is how it's going to affect us tonight," said Charles after a silence that had gone on too long. " Only your father can decide that for us, Isabella—nobody else knows where the pictures are."

" They'll be in the older part of the house," she said slowly. " There's one wing they don't use now—part of it was the nursery when we were there, and rooms for spinster aunts, and so on, that's where I think the pictures are."

" I noticed the wall," said Harry. " Does it run all round the place?"

" Yes, I'm afraid it does."

" Too bad. We've got ourselves a job, if those front gates are locked. The place is a fort, not a country house."

Isabella looked at Harry. " My father knows another way in. It will be all right."

" I'm relieved," said Harry flatly. " Climbing a fifteen foot wall isn't for me." He smiled and added : " I haven't the build."

" Why were they put up, Isabella?" Charles asked.

" We had an eccentric ancestor," she said. " About 1830, I believe. There had been some popular risings and he got the idea that the local peasants might one day attack him. So he had the walls built. He must have been quite mad and there was never any trouble. But the walls were there and nobody bothered to have them pulled down; the trees hide them from the house mostly; in fact you can climb the wall by the trees in lots of places—the village boys do when the fruit is ripe, or they used to. I don't think you'll find the walls a very serious obstacle tonight."

Her last remarks were aimed at Harry. She was still giving him her charming hostess smile; a little cool and formal, perhaps.

" I hope you're right," said Harry.

9

THEY WERE drowsy after lunch behind shuttered windows; with cigarettes and coffee their conversation had dribbled away and Harry was demonstrably half-asleep, his bulky frame sprawling uncomfortably in the room's only approximation to an easy chair; from the wide empty fireplaces a dark smoke-blackened Crucifix brooded over them; in her kitchen Eulalia was crooning a lament in a throaty contralto about *malherida España*, sorely-wounded Spain and her many griefs.

Just before three o'clock they set out, Charles, Harry, and José. Isabella had decided she didn't need to be with them since José knew the neighbourhood even better than she did : anything they wanted to know José could tell them.

"*Perfectamente*," said José and he was pleased beyond words when the Señorita Isabella lent him her father's binoculars.

Isabella warned them that they'd have a rough climb if José took the goat track and José nodded his head and showed his teeth : not for nothing was the land called *La Montana*—there were hills everywhere.

"It had come to our notice," said Charles and gave it up in the face of José's enthusiasm.

"It wouldn't be any good trying to take the car," said

Isabella. " You'd have to drive a long way round and even then you wouldn't be able to reach the place José wants on the side of the valley—you can see most of the house from there—and I don't think it would be a good idea for your car to be noticed too much down there. We don't get many tourists as far off the map as this."

" So we walk," said Charles cheerfully.

After half an hour at a brisk pace they were climbing among rocks on the side of a hill and even the goat track had disappeared. The sun beat down on them and the flat surfaces of rock made their fingers tingle; for most of the way there was very little shade and not much in the way of a foothold.

José's agility was enviable: his ungainly stride, knees bent and body leaning forward, took him over the steep broken ground at a deceptively steady pace; Harry War-render soon gave up cursing the heat and the rocks and the general impossibility of the terrain: he was fully extended keeping up.

Charles was coping rather better than he had expected, apart from the feeling of being broiled alive whenever they found themselves flattened on an exposed outcrop of rock, working their way foot by foot, often on hands and knees.

José remained encouraging and provocatively cheerful. This was less than nothing to him.

They were coming slowly and diagonally round the slope of a hill, and there was more shade there and the beginnings of a shallow valley below and some woodland opposite.

José halted and pointed, pleased with himself. In the trees across the little valley they could see part of a house and windows shimmering in the sun. The further round they went the more the view opened.

Five minutes later José waved his hand in a gesture that plainly said: Here we are. His observation post was surrounded by bushes on three sides and gave a view of much of the house opposite on the other. Beyond it the hill began to bend away again. Without crossing the valley this seemed to be as near as you could get to the house; there were some sun-dried cigarette ends on the ground just below the rocky ledge that served as a parapet.

They couldn't see all of the house because of the trees; as an architect Charles Connell found its mixture of styles oddly fascinating: it was as though successive Mundayas had set out to show how little each had cared for the deplorable taste of his predecessor; the roofs were on varying levels; chunks had been added on here and there without balance or proportion.

They could see some lawns and hedges and part of bright flowerbeds; down below them in the trees was a stretch of the wall, little more than a hundred yards away; it didn't look very formidable and the trees were growing close up against it.

Harry Warrender found a shady spot, took off his shoes and emptied the dust out of them disgustedly.

"We've had the exercise," he said. "I will now recuperate while you examine what you can see of your beloved's ancestral home. Wake me if there's a crisis." He stretched out and closed his eyes.

José was squatting by the rock parapet with the binoculars; there was nothing stirring. Charles offered him a cigarette and they smoked in silence while the heat shimmered over the valley. Charles tried the glasses and the lawns and the flower bed moved up to him and he could almost count the slats on one of the shuttered windows and the steps that led down from the terrace to the lawns.

José finished his cigarette, touched him lightly on the arm and said:

"*Espere por favor, Señor.*" And it was clear from the gesture that went with it that José was inviting him to stay put please.

Charles nodded and José slipped down between the bushes, waved, and disappeared among the trees.

"*Mañana, mañana,* its wonderful," said Harry lazily. "Has the lad abandoned us?"

"Gone for a closer look, I think." Charles tried to pick up some signs of José's progress below, but even with the binoculars he found nothing to indicate that José was down there.

"He won't find out anything we didn't know already." Harry yawned. "The lady is there with her heart-throb while hubbie goes to work. Barcelona, was it? That makes it safe enough."

"Perhaps they're not stopping," said Charles. "We need to know that."

Harry turned on his side, cushioning his head on his arm. He smiled. "What a nice earnest mind you have, Charles. Of *course* they'll stop the night—why pay hotel bills?"

Some twenty minutes went by; Harry had exhausted his speculation about the extra-marital habits of Señora Ludmilla Carceres; Charles spasmodically watched the valley and tried to picture the shapeless house opposite as it had been when Isabella was a baby—she had probably crawled on that very stretch of lawn he could see below the terrace, perhaps one of those square windows with the green shutters looked in on her nursery; she must have been little more than a year old when they left to come to England—

and now old Luis had come back to spend the rest of his days in an obscure cottage within a few miles of the place that had been his and his ancestors' for generations, and Charles Connell was going to marry his daughter—

A sudden moving colour caught his eye and he raised the glasses again. There was a small flat roof topping one of the old additions to the main building. A woman in a bright red wrap had come out on to it from a tall window; her hair was a brilliant blonde, dazzling in the sun, matching the white frame of her sunglasses; behind her came a tall young man in a coloured loose shirt worn outside a pair of dark trunks; over his arm he carried a folded rug and on his wrist Charles caught the glint of a watch strap or bracelet; he was smoking a cigarette in a thin white holder and Charles could clearly see the lazy drifting of the smoke in the air.

The young man spread the rug on the roof; the woman shook her brilliant hair back and slipped off her wrap.

She might well be known locally as the French tart, Charles reflected, but her body was certainly very beautiful: slender and pale brown except for the tiny bikini coverings in white that helped to make her appear more naked than if she had been wearing nothing at all. She was sitting on the rug and the young man was kneeling beside her rubbing her shoulders with suntan lotion and when she reached back and removed her brassière he went on rubbing and he was making a very careful job of it; then he whipped the colourful shirt over his head and the lady oiled him in his turn : his trunk was dark and muscular and hairless and while she worked over him he flexed himself and Charles saw his mouth open in a laugh, and his companion rocked against him, her forehead against his shoulder. They were very good friends indeed.

The flat roof couldn't be overlooked from the house, and the pair of sunbathers had no reason, clearly, not to behave as though they were in complete privacy; the young man went in through the window and came back in a moment with a large towel, brightly striped, a scarlet straw hat and some cushions. They made themselves comfortable and the lady wore the straw hat; she toasted her back and shoulders for minutes and then rolled lazily over.

Charles lowered his glasses. This was something Harry would like very much; he used to tell a very circumstantial story of the time he had rented a room on the inside court-yard of a hotel block and used to watch a couple making love on the floor below opposite.

Charles lit another cigarette and stubbed it out almost immediately; in the last few days he had been far exceeding his quota and the ulcer would be protesting, quite apart from the unfamiliar diet. Harry was really sleeping now; if he knew what he was missing he wouldn't be terribly cordial. Charles let him sleep. Without bothering with the glasses he knew the sunbathers were still on the roof and occupied with more than the healing rays of the sun.

José climbed up into view, looking hot and damp but happy and full of news.

Automóvil figured in his report and *Señorita Carceres,* but most of it was lost on them.

Harry roused himself, noticed the woman on the roof and grabbed the glasses. The scarlet wrap was back in place and its owner was going inside.

" How long has she been out there, Charles?" Harry asked. " Did you see her?"

" I did," said Charles, " and her boy friend. They've been sunbathing for the last forty minutes or so. While you slept. I imagine she is Señora Carceres."

José watched the lady disappear.

" *Hijo de puta!* " said José forcefully.

" I gather that translates as ' dirty tart '," said Harry. " I think you're all being a little rough on the lady—and you're a louse to keep it all to yourself, Charles."

" You've seen a woman in a bikini before," said Charles, " even with the top missing."

" Shameful," said Harry cheerfully. " I'm sorry you didn't wake me."

They started the climb back, and it took them longer than before; José didn't press them so hard and proved amenable when Charles indicated that it might be time for a short rest now and then; there was a faint breeze that fanned the tops of the trees and took the fierce edge off the heat; they met some tethered goats in a small clearing, and Harry slipped and scraped his forearm on a sloping ledge of rock; in his expressed opinion the afternoon had been a waste of time and Charles had to remind him that they did not yet know what José might have discovered. Hearing his name quoted José looked back at them and smiled and said : " *Muy bueno!* "

They got back to the house; Eulalia was absent, still at her *siesta*; so they sat in the cool kitchen and pumped water into a bucket and José told Isabella all about it.

He had been over the wall and he had talked with old Garcia whose daughter had married a cousin of José's and whose information could thus be taken as reliable; Garcia did odd jobs outside in the grounds but spent all the time he could in the kitchens, both for food and the snippets of gossip that enlivened his existence. And there was plenty of gossip about Señora Ludmilla Carceres; she and her lover were certainly spending the night there and there would be only two servants left in the house, both female and at least one of them was no better than she need be if all Garcia heard was to be believed, but then what could one expect from an ignorant young trollop from Reinosa in a household where the Señora herself was no better than a whore for all her French scents and fashions? Sweet Mother of God, Juan Carceres was no *caballero*, but even he deserved a better wife than Ludmilla Carceres.

The young man with her this time was a French dancer and play-actor from San Sebastian and this was not the first time he had been there, though never before as the sole guest and with Señor Carceres away.

José went out to see to the milking of his few cows; Eulalia appeared and firmly desired their absence from her kitchen because she for one had work to do; she broke into one of her melancholy litanies and won her point with ease. Isabella took them out to a small patch of rough grass shaded by the corner of the house where they had the track up to the farm in full view from where it left the wood.

Harry had listened to Isabella's translation of José's report with an amused smile and it wasn't difficult to guess on which side his sympathy really lay, but Charles was glad that he didn't say anything argumentative beyond remarking that the two of them might well have saved themselves the climb.

When Luis Mundaya at last appeared at the bottom of the track Isabella went to meet him; he was walking slowly and stiffly and using his stick, the hunched left shoulder pulling his head to one side.

Harry Warrender watched him greet his daughter and link his arm in hers and they heard the two of them laugh.

" Cagey old bird," Harry said softly. " Puts on a good act."

" He's a fine man," said Charles. " I don't think I've ever met anyone with so much character. And guts. Look what he's been through."

" Maybe," said Harry.

" There's no maybe about it." The sudden heat in his voice made Harry smile with surprise.

Charles went on, in a quieter voice : " Nothing in the world would make him surrender his principles—and his whole life has been a proof of it."

" I'd like to have asked his wife what she thought," said Harry. " It can be a little rough being married to an idealist. I wonder what she felt about her old man chucking everything overboard for the sake of politics—what the hell difference does it make in the long run? Anyone could see Franco was going to win and the Fascists and Nazis backed him. Old Luis Mundaya let himself get left behind. And now look at him, damn nearly a pauper. All those years in jail—and what for? What good did it do anybody? Have you ever asked Isabella what she thought?"

" I wouldn't need to. I know. And so do you, Harry."

" I wouldn't be too sure," said Harry bleakly. " Fanaticism may be all right as long as it doesn't involve other people—personally I prefer to keep Number One in the front of my mind."

They went down to meet Isabella and her father. Although Luis was moving slowly and carefully he showed no sign of distress after his walk; in spite of his frailness there was a toughness in him that would drive his body forward long after most men in his condition would have given up.

His visit to the padre in the village had not been entirely social.

" For a holy old man Bartolomeo is a great gossip,"

said Luis as they came up the slope under the olives. "You would be surprised how much the village knows already about you two gentlemen. The general opinion is that you are both mad to be sleeping in tents when you obviously have the money to go to a hotel in a town, but then in these parts we still expect Englishmen to be eccentric. There is nothing for us to be alarmed about and you will be gone by tomorrow; they may talk among themselves but you can be sure nothing will reach anybody in authority: the *Guardia Civil* post for instance. We have a long tradition of non-co-operation with the police." He smiled. "I am part of that tradition myself, I fear."

When they told him about the presence of Señora Ludmilla Carceres and her escort his comment was characteristic: "We should have expected something like that, but we must not let it interfere with us. Now will you gentlemen join me in a *fino* to see the sun down? We have plans to make and time runs on."

10

It was half past eleven; they were sitting round the bare oak table in the lamplight; José was with them; he wore a dark jersey and dark serge trousers that had been his best wear for many years; he was smoking a long pale brown cigar and listening respectfully to conversations that he didn't understand; all he knew was that something was happening that night with the Señor and his English friends and that the Señor had said he would be grateful for José's assistance when the time came; and that had been enough for José.

Luis had drawn a map, and he was explaining how they were going to get in without having to climb any walls in the dark.

" When my father was a young man the life of a Spanish gentleman was pretty rigidly supervised, at least until he married and set up his own establishment; if you were lucky and your parents had the money you might manage the odd visit to Paris or Nice with a liberal-minded tutor and amuse yourself while you were there and until papa called you back. My own grandparents were really of the old school and I gather father had a fairly thin time; in most of the rooms smoking was absolutely forbidden by my grandmother and she was the complete autocrat: she had brought money into the family and I can't think she ever let grandfather forget it—he had to go to his own study to enjoy a cigar after dinner. It all sounds pretty grim and rigid to us. Now if you will look at this sketch you will see where I have marked the old stables and you'll notice that the wall is less than fifty yards away at that point—elsewhere it's as much as half a mile from the house. But at that place behind the stables the wall had to swing inwards, otherwise it would have had to span the stream below. You see? And then it would have had to cross the stream again further down to get back. Well, my father discovered a way out of the grounds: there's an underground passage from the stables that comes out in a thicket just above the stream. As far as I can discover the passage must have been built about the time the Moors were overrunning Asturias; there must have been some kind of a fort here, where the stables were built later. Probably the passage was designed to enable a besieged garrison to crawl out at night for water from the stream or send scouts for help. They built it well and it's still there. José and I crawled along it a month ago."

"Father!" said Isabella reprovingly.

He smiled. "It was a godsend to my father. It was far more romantic to slip out at night by an underground passage than to creep down through the gardens and the drive and climb the gates—which were always locked at sunset and guarded by a lodge-keeper. Father was quite discreet, but I gather he had some pretty wild nights once he found the passage."

"I can imagine," said Harry Warrender. "And how close can we bring the car?"

Luis Mundaya traced the route with his pencil on the sketch he had made, and Harry studied it carefully; most of the way would be by rough cart tracks over which it wouldn't be possible to hurry.

" I have another useful piece of information," said Luis. " This time from my good friend Bartolomeo : our local policeman left on his bicycle to investigate a stabbing affray among some gipsies up in the hills; it will certainly take him most of the night. It's comforting to know he'll be out of the way since he takes his duties more seriously than most of his colleagues : he has an unpleasant habit of cycling round at night when all sensible policemen should be in bed and asleep; he's new to the district, I believe, a foreigner from Burgos."

Luis broke off and said something in Spanish to José; José smiled and replied and whipped his forefinger across his throat and Luis Mundaya laughed.

" José says the first dark night he meets that policeman will be his last," Luis translated cheerfully and smiled when Isabella patted him on the shoulder and told him he ought to be ashamed of himself, at his age, to be so lawless.

Luis laughed aloud delightedly. " All my life has been one of rigorous rectitude ! As for that villain José : Eulalia prays for his unregenerate soul every time she goes to church and that is often enough." He was in a very good humour, there was even a faint hint of colour in his tight thin cheeks; the night's adventure that lay ahead seemed to have taken years off his age; Charles noticed that he had drunk nothing beyond a single glass of sherry earlier in the evening; it wasn't impossible to see how even years of privation in prison had failed to defeat him.

Charles experienced an extraordinary feeling of strange affection for the white haired old man with the crippled arm and the indomitable spirit; Harry called him a crazy fanatic who didn't know when he'd been beaten and who refused to face up to reality—Charles wondered just how far Harry really thought that; all the evening Harry had said very little and he had been careful with his drinking, even refusing the brandy, but he had been smoking endlessly and automatically. Once or twice Charles had caught him watching Isabella with more intentness than good manners, but there was nothing to be done about that. That was just Harry being himself—and in the soft amber lamplight Isabella was worth looking at with the quiet grace of her movement and the way the brilliant smile enlivened her face as she talked and joked with her father.

Charles was looking at the sketch. Luis had made no attempt to draw the house; he had marked it just as an irregular oblong somewhere near the old stables.

"We've had the underground passage," Harry said, dribbling smoke out of his mouth as he spoke. "Do we now come to the sliding panels, sir?" He was smiling, his flushed heavy face partly in shadow. "I've been hoping for something more original."

Luis Mundaya nodded. "And I think you will have it, Mr. Warrender—we will do our best not to disappoint you when we get there." His voice was pleasant, polite; the thin fingers of his right hand played on the table in the pool of light. "We will need tools with us. José has them ready."

"He's coming inside with us?" Harry asked. "Will that be safe?"

"It is fortunate for you, Mr. Warrender, that José does not understand what we are saying. It was José's father who hid the pictures with me. He died in prison."

Harry shifted in his seat. "I spoke out of turn. I'm sorry, sir."

"It is nothing; you didn't know. There will be work for the four of us tonight—three men and an old cripple

G

like me." Luis Mundaya stood up, drew Isabella towards him and kissed her. "We are leaving now, my dear. You had better go to bed. This will possibly take us two hours, with luck."

She linked her arm with his. "You don't really think I could sleep while all this is going on, do you? I'd love to be coming with you. I'll have coffee ready and a lamp in the window."

Outside in the darkness Charles managed to get Harry on his own for a moment as Harry bent at the rear of the Humber for a final check; they had already taken out most of the packing to make room for the pictures and when they got the pictures in place they were to come back and re-place the packing so that there'd be no rattle or damaging movement to the canvas or frames.

"Harry," said Charles quietly. "You brought a gun, didn't you?"

Squatting on his heels Harry looked up at him. "How did you know?"

"Last night," said Charles. "I saw you."

Harry laughed softly, straightening up. "You're sharper than I thought, Charles. Well?"

"We agreed," said Charles patiently. "No guns, Harry. Right?"

"Maybe I changed my mind."

"And it wasn't important enough to tell me," Charles said. "Why?"

"You're giving yourself the answer. You're fussing over something that doesn't matter, Charles. I knew you would. That's why I didn't tell you. Don't build up a thing about it, old boy, not now."

"Where is the gun. It's not in the car. I looked."

"In my pocket," said Harry softly, "and there's just

nothing you can do about it—it might even come in handy." He walked round to the front of the Humber.

José rode in the back and whatever tools he had were wrapped in a dark cloth. There was no moon, a clear star-lit night, very still and mild; no breeze in the dark trees.

Harry drove carefully and gently, with one dimmed headlamp, coasting whenever possible in complete quietness down below the trees; under Luis Mundaya's direction they avoided the small sleeping village, making a wide irregular detour that took them along bumpy rutted tracks with the coarse grass and weeds axle-high. Later Harry said he was able to do without even the one dimmed headlight as they rolled quietly along a narrow lane with high banks on each side; the side lights alone were enough.

Over the bump of a bridge they rocked down between the tall crowding trunks of a coppice and Harry found he needed all the light he had. Then began the difficult part of the drive: grinding and bumping over broken ground that was never meant for wheeled traffic; at one spot under the trees Harry had to back and heave at the wheel to find a way through without running up against the trunk of a tree or an overgrown boulder; and some of the gradients had him swearing softly with the entire approval of his passengers in the front seat; José was being tossed from side to side but made no complaint.

They got out on to the grass. It was very dark now after the Humber's lights had been switched off; the only sound was the clicking of the engine as it cooled down after all that work in low gear.

There was a steep overgrown bank sliding down to the bed of the stream where there was very little water; the heavy covering of the wood pressed in on them, masking most of the sky; the wall was a dark mass in front and above them, merging into the tangle of the trees, quite lost in the overpowering blackness.

" We follow José," Luis Mundaya whispered.

José had a shaded torch. Bending double he was pushing his way through the bushes, pausing now and then to let them catch up. The thicket seemed endless, specially designed to tear all the skin off face and hands and then blind one for good measure.

José was squatting in a small opening, carefully lifting loose stones away one at a time and placing them on the grass. When he judged the hole big enough he shone his torch in the opening.

" *Buena suerte,*" he murmured. Good luck.

Harry climbed in after him, then Charles, and lastly Luis Mundaya who had so far survived the ordeal very well and said he felt fine.

The tunnel sloped upwards. For the most part it was about four feet high with roughly bricked sides that had caved in here and there so that they had to crawl on hands and knees. The footing was very fair, all in all, and it was dry except at the lower end; the air was stale and earthly and thick, but by no means foul as it might have been. There had evidently been some recent attempts at clearing a way through the growths that sprouted from the bricks and brushed their faces unpleasantly in the dark.

This was where Luis Mundaya was beginning to feel the pace; Charles could hear him snatching at his breath, like a fighter taking heavy punishment.

" Are you all right, sir? Would you like to rest?" he asked.

"No, my dear boy, no—just keep on—I'll be all right—
we're over halfway—!" Luis Mundaya was panting labori-
ously, handicapped by being able to use only his right arm
to support himself against the wall and help himself up-
ward. "Go on, Charles!" he insisted. "This is a one-way
street!"

At the top where the passage widened out they waited
for him and José whispered: "*Que tal,* Señor Luis?"

Luis Mundaya climbed the last few yards and said with
emphasis: "*Bueno!*"

After all that exertion the exit was easy. José braced
himself with his hands flat against a stone slab over his
head. It lifted from its bed with no trouble and he slid
it to one side and pulled himself up; it was a narrow opening but quite wide enough for a man's body. He helped
the other three up and he was very gentle indeed with
Señor Luis, making him sit for some minutes on a pile of
timber until he recovered himself; they were all travel-
stained and very grubby; it was a relief to be able to stand
upright and stretch.

Harry lit a cigarette but José came over and took it from
him politely and trod it underfoot, murmuring: "*Por favor
Señor—*"

They were in a small lofty windowless room with dim
high rafters and peeling walls; it was littered with pieces
of old rotting timber, odds and ends of harness and saddlery
green with age and neglect, dusty bottles, old straw and
sacking; in the corner the curved wooden ribs of a manger
were heaped with rusted tins; the wall over the opening
where they had emerged bulged crazily out and the old
plaster flaked and crumbled as soon as you touched it;
there was one low arched doorway, but no door.

Harry wiped his smeared hands on the seat of his trousers.

"Exciting," he said, "but I'd rather go down than up."

Luis Mundaya sat resting with his one good hand on his knee; he had collected a lot of dirt during the climb.

"My apologies for holding the party up," he said pleasantly as though they were on a purely social occasion. "In a moment we will begin the really interesting part of our expedition. The pictures are in the kitchen in the older part of the house. We have to move a large dresser and then José will loosen the masonry up near the ceiling, and we will find what we want."

"If somebody hasn't been there first," said Harry softly.

Luis Mundaya lifted his head. "They were there a month ago. I saw them. We could have taken them then but there were only the two of us, and we were on foot—I preferred to wait until I had better plans for their disposal —such as with the help of you two enterprising and willing gentlemen. Are you satisfied, Mr. Warrender?" Luis Mundaya's voice was without emotion, but with just a trace of weariness. And he plainly wasn't expecting any answer.

He got to his feet and held out his hand and José gave him the torch.

"We shall be going through a courtyard to the carriage way and behind the gardens," said Luis. "Once we are outside I will not be able to use the torch and we will walk on the grass wherever possible."

"Any dogs?" Charles asked.

"No dogs. No horses. Carceres has no sporting tastes. There is a deaf couple living in the coach house outside here, two indoor servants as we know. And the Carceres woman and her lover. It is a big house and I know my way. Unless we are very clumsy—or unlucky—we should have no trouble."

They moved out, Luis Mundaya leading and José at his shoulder; as Charles accidentally bumped against Harry going through the arched door he felt the sharp bulge of the gun in Harry's pocket. Then they were outside and in the darkness.

11

THEY CROSSED the cobbled courtyard, came out under a wide arch, and moved across a patch of dark even grass to a high wall and then a white fence beyond which was the quiet unlit mass of the house; there was some gravel that they couldn't avoid and the four of them crunched over it as gently as they could.

They were at the side of the house, somewhere at the back; there was a heavy door, iron-studded, and some high windows; Luis Mundaya shone his torch over the windows and found one that was open at the top; it was just out of reach.

José whispered something and Luis said to Harry: " Give José a lift, will you—then he can let us in."

Harry bent with his hands against the wall and José climbed on his shoulders and very quietly eased the window up. He disappeared inside, and a few moments later the door was opening; it was old and heavy and its hinges needed oiling.

There were four stone steps and a wide corridor. They left the door open behind them.

"Remember the steps," said Luis softly, "when you carry the pictures out. There's just one more step further up in front of us. We turn left and we are in the kitchen. There are no carpets or mats down here, just stone floors

—the kitchen is still furnished but they don't use it any more."

It was a vast dim room with three small windows; the cooking smells of the past still hung in the air and even in the dark you couldn't mistake what the room had been; slap in the middle of the room there was a solid table thick enough to serve as a butcher's block; there was a stone sink and a long-handled pump and a large unpolished wood-burning stove; a massive dark dresser covered almost all of one wall, reaching to the ceiling.

"Good God," Harry Warrender whispered, "we don't have to shift that I hope?"

Luis Mundaya laughed softly and led the way into a smaller room opening off the main kitchen. There were shelves all around with glasses and some crockery; it was all very dusty; a smaller dresser sat against one wall.

Luis shone his torch over it and said:

"There we are, gentlemen. We move that first of all."

Inch by inch they moved the dresser away from the wall; some abandoned cutlery rattled in one of the drawers and Charles Connell took it out and put it all on a shelf; José unwrapped his tools: a chisel and a small hammer with its head bound round with cloth. He climbed up on the dresser, put the torch on the top so that it lit up the wall just under the ceiling, and began a very careful tapping with his hammer.

The wall was rough brick with no plaster surface and the bricks were loose.

"The floor above is on two levels," said Luis Mundaya, "and there's a gap of at least two feet between the ceiling there and the floor above—when José's father and I hid the pictures we used mortar when we replaced the bricks,

but last month when José and I came here José loosened
the plaster and filled in with putty."

" Which he happened to have in his pocket," said Harry.
" Very convenient."

" Not at all," said Luis pleasantly. " We were prepared,
Mr. Warrender—that shouldn't surprise you, should it?"

José was removing the bricks one by one and placing
them on top of the dresser; he was methodical and quite
unhurried. Very soon he had an opening almost a foot deep
and over a yard wide just below the ceiling.

" We must organise ourselves," Luis Mundaya whispered.
" I think Jose manages the tunnel better than any of us—
we will take the pictures to the top of the tunnel and José
will get them down."

" Do it faster if there were two of us on it," Harry said,
" obviously. I could team up with José—at least I ought to
be there at the bottom to stow them away in the car."

" All right," said Luis. " Then Charles and I can clear
up here. We don't want to leave any trace of our visit."

" I can lay a brick," said Charles. " It wouldn't be the
first."

José reached into the opening and lifted out a flat pack-
age sewn-up in sacking and he was smiling as he handed
it down. Two more followed, all the same size and weight,
and wrapped in the same way.

Luis beckoned José down and explained. José nodded.

" I can carry one to the tunnel," Charles said, " then
come back here and tidy up."

They left Luis Mundaya on his own in the kitchen with
the torch. The pictures in their wrappings were just a little
too bulky to be carried comfortably under the arm : two
hands were needed to keep them steady.

Charles had an unhappy vision of stumbling in the dark

and putting his foot through that precious square of canvas; the scrambling journey down through the tunnel was going to be particularly hazardous; two of them holding a picture between them and working as a team might manage it—if one of them didn't miss his footing and fall over.

And that was the way Harry and José decided to try it when they reached the old stables.

" We'll do the three together," said Harry, " one flat on top of the other."

He struck a match and demonstrated what he meant. José hunched his broad shoulders, waved his hands and nodded. He was to go first.

Charles watched them start. José at least would be careful and take no risks with their cargo. For a few minutes he listened to the sounds of their descent. There was some language from Harry but nothing from José.

Charles went back to the house. Luis Mundaya was waiting in the kitchen, sitting on the heavy table, his shoulders drooping.

" They're all right," said Charles.

" Good." Luis Mundaya's voice was very soft. He sounded tired and his movements were stiff as he got to his feet and led the way back to finish the job.

Charles climbed up on the dresser and started replacing the bricks loose, fitting one against another as well as he could. It wouldn't stand any kind of inspection now, but that didn't matter. It took him ten careful minutes before he was satisfied.

When he got down he collected the fragments of mortar and dried putty from the floor in his handkerchief, opened the window and scattered them outside.

Then he and Luis pushed the dresser back into place against the wall.

"Back to normal, sir," said Charles. "A complete success, I think."

Luis Lundaya touched his arm. "Thank you, Charles."

They went out into the corridor beyond the large deserted kitchen. But instead of turning towards the door Luis Mundaya paused.

"Charles," he murmured. "I doubt if I will visit here again—the Mundayas lived here so long: I would like to show you a little of the house. It was Isabella's home when she was a baby and I have very happy memories here still."

"I'd like that," Charles said softly.

They were in a wide corridor, thickly carpeted; the wallpaper was heavily embossed, and there were some elegantly panelled doors in finely grained woods. Some of the proportions were finer than Charles had expected, especially the lofty grace of the hall and main staircase with its slender curved rail and delicate tracery in cream wrought-iron.

They were in the middle of the hall. Luis said he would show him the library and music room.

"Madame Patti herself sang there," he whispered. "It was a beautiful room—"

The lights in the chandelier overhead came on with a sudden blinding brilliance, and for a frozen moment nobody moved.

At the top of the stairs there was a young man in a cream robe with a brilliant red sash; he was very swarthy and the robe made him look almost a negro; a handsome arrogant young men. And not in the least afraid of the intruders: he had a gun in his hand. Just behind him in a pale blue robe held high up against her throat was the lady of the house, Ludmilla Carceres herself.

The young man said nothing. He pointed the gun and

fired quite deliberately. Glass shattered somewhere in the front of the hall. And the echoes were still ringing when Ludmilla Carceres screamed. The young man smiled and fired again. He was enjoying this. He was aiming down the stairs, the skirts of his robe parting to show brown muscular naked legs.

Charles grabbed Luis Mundaya by the shoulder and dragged him back in to the corridor and for a few yards the old man was quite fast.

Ludmilla Carceres came stumbling down the stairs, her arms outstretched, and caught her lover round the waist. Charles scooped up a vase with some tall purple flowers and hurled it at the stairs and hit the young man in the chest. He saw him fall in an untidy muddle with the lady on top of him and Ludmilla Carceres stopped screaming abruptly with her legs thrashing the air ungracefully.

Charles thundered down the carpeted corridor. In the blaze of light from the hall he could still see Luis Mundaya in front of him. They had to be out of the house before that trigger-happy young man got after them.

He caught up with Luis before they reached the old kitchen and Charles had slammed every door they went through but none of them had keys or bolts on the helpful side. If that young man caught up with them in a corridor—

Luis Mundaya was leaning against the wall with his head bowed, fighting painfully and noisily for breath. A spasm of dry coughing shook him and bent him over, and Charles had to hold him with an arm around his shoulders. They had dropped to little more than a slow shuffling walk and the door they wanted seemed to come no nearer.

"You go!" Luis Mundaya panted. "You go, Charles— I'll talk to that young fool with a gun—!"

"You can make it—we'll be all right when we get outside." Charles was half-carrying the old man. "Just hang on to me—" All the time he was listening for noises in the rear—and praying for Harry and José to arrive.

They staggered down the four steps, through the open door and out into the shelter of the darkness. Luis had recovered himself but he was quite unable to run any more and the best he could manage was a shambling sort of trot, holding on to Charles's arm, with frequent pauses while he fought for breath and tried in vain to stop the coughing that racked him and had him reeling blindly against Charles with his hands groping for support.

They were coming up to the open archway into the courtyard when Charles heard the sounds behind them and a quick beam of light jerked about, looking for them, lighting up the high blank wall and the arch and the empty windows of the coachhouse. And then the two of them, just a few yards short of the shelter of the arch and the wall.

Charles half-turned, blinded by the torch and raised his hand.

"Stop!" he shouted. And in that instant the young man fired and brick dust spurted on the wall full in the beam of light. And behind them the man laughed and called out something.

Luis Mundaya swayed through the archway, his thin legs spread apart and the light caught his bobbing white head. He was nearly round the corner. Two more steps and he would be away from the light.

It was suicide to stand and shout. Charles caught a momentary glimpse of Luis Mundaya's face. There were two quick shots. He felt a sharp slap in his left side that spun him round and toppled him to the ground. He was on

his knees wondering what he had run into, and he heard
the thud of running feet and although there was something
strange happening to his sight he recognised José running
past him, crouching and running full in the light.

And a voice was saying: "Hurry up, Harry, and bring
that blasted gun—" It must have been his own voice because there was nobody else.

He heard one more shot and the light jerked off. There
were some grunts and the scraping of feet.

Charles was managing to stand upright, but not easily.

The whole of his left side, from armpit to thigh, seemed
frozen, numb. No pain. Just a feeling that he didn't have
a left side any more. And when he touched himself he knew
the stickiness must be blood.

José was back, whispering: "Señor Luis—Señor Luis—"
Harshly, urgently.

With his left elbow tucked against his side Charles was
trying to walk.

"José—"

José was carrying something slung over his shoulder and
it wasn't until he came up so close that he could touch him
that Charles knew it was Luis Mundaya José carried.

It was then that Charles found his breathing becoming
difficult and his legs uncertain all of a sudden as though
he were wading knee-deep in mud. And when he held his
face he felt the frightening chill of his own sweat.

"José," he mumbled, "I don't think I can—"

He was bumping against things, trying to follow José,
and he was trying not to breathe because every breath now
was worse than the one before—red hot stabbing through
his side—and the sobbing he was hearing couldn't possibly
be himself.

José was saying something and once he blundered into

him and felt Luis Mundaya's bony skin through his trousers. But he was moving, still moving and keeping up—

They were inside. José had found the torch in Luis Mundaya's pocket and he had taken off the piece of cloth that dimmed it; he had Luis Mundaya stretched on the floor with his head resting in his lap and he was whispering words that Charles couldn't hear because of the strange rushing in his ears like a waterfall.

A misty sort of curtain kept clouding his eyes and anything he tried to touch was made of soft velvet or else it wasn't there at all.

There was one moment of clarity when the mists rolled back and he saw Luis Mundaya's sightless eyes as José carried the body over to the opening down into the tunnel.

" He's dead, José," he said. " Can't you see he's dead?" It seemed to him important to establish that fact, in case José had overlooked it.

Either José didn't hear him, or else he hadn't actually spoken at all. It was odd. The floor was moving up and down so he had to crawl to the edge of the hole. It was still more odd to see José waiting for him and holding him back and pulling up his shirt, and then José was pulling off his jersey and ripping his shirt off and tearing it into strips, whispering something at him all the time and smiling at him as though they shared a secret.

He could smell José's strong sweat, and that was a comfort because it meant he wasn't on his own. The stone floor was cold under his back where José had lifted his shirt and loosened the waist of his trousers.

The pain in his side was quite definite now: sharp, rhythmical, catching his breathing.

José had a dagger tattooed just above his navel and it

wrinkled as he bent. He was making a firm bandage and when he had finished he tapped Charles lightly on the jaw with his clenched fist and grinned, kneeling up and pulling on his jersey.

"*Muy hombre!*"

"You're quite an *hombre* yourself." Charles pushed himself up on one hand, his right hand. The bandage was tight, but it certainly helped. His left arm was covered in blood from the elbow down. He was concentrating, catching the rhythm of the pain so that he could be ready for it each time—he was wondering how much blood he could lose and remain even partially conscious.

He heard himself saying: "Harry—where's Harry—?"

José shook his head and spread his hands expressively. And said nothing.

Getting down into the tunnel was bad. It stretched his side viciously and he had to let himself fall into Jose's arms. It was hell.

José had the old man propped against the ledge. He gave Charles the torch and pointed downwards. He caught the body of Luis Mundaya under the armpits; there wasn't room to carry it and he was going to let the legs trail. So he must be dead.

Charles started down very slowly, sideways, like a crab, favouring his left side; José was moving backwards and his broad shoulders filled the tunnel.

For a very short while Charles almost thought he was going to make it; he was isolating the pain in his mind, clamping his jaws hard each time it came, not breathing, forcing himself to accept it as something that wasn't permanent and thus mustn't be allowed to beat him—but it was like no other pain he had ever known in all his life

H

and its sharpness was increasing and driving the sweat down his face.

He knew he was bleeding again through the bandage José had fixed. When he started to miss his footing and fall he knew he wasn't going to make it to the bottom. Fainting was a queer sensation—soft, swimming, almost pleasant, floating upwards in softness, not even any need now to hold your breath—just everything floating around. Quiet and dark. No pain.

12

He was alone and it was dark. He felt cold and yet there seemed to be a fire burning all over him. All kinds of crazy things were happening to him : he was riding a horse over a limitless field, shouting: "Harry! Harry! Where the hell are you?" And in the middle of it the horse tossed him and he was falling for ever and ever.

It was quite crazy and it made him shiver. Nothing that was happening had any connection with anything else—and some of the pictures dancing in front of him were so vivid that he knew they must be happening to somebody else. Or else he was really dead.

He didn't ever want to move. In the dark. It must be death. It couldn't be anything else. He wanted to laugh because it wasn't at all what he had thought it would be and there were so many other things he wanted to do—and he wanted to tell somebody. Isabella. He began very carefully to explain to Isabella that he didn't have much time and it wasn't his fault. His mouth wasn't behaving—like having your jaw frozen at the dentist's. But he had to tell Isabella before it was too late.

There was some light somewhere, like staring into the sun until it hurt. And people talking a long way off. Then the floating sensation. And a stab of pain that cut everything off. This was the real thing at last. There could be no doubt about it—

It was extraordinary that he could still feel movement that tipped him up and down, and all he wanted was to let the blackness roll over him.

The first thing he saw was a thick whitewashed beam sloping down over his head. White, clear white. No blackness anywhere. There was a firm softness under his head. Cool. No galloping horses. Nobody shouting for *Harry*.

The pain in his side was rising and rising and he knew it would never stop. Because it was that kind of pain. Just devouring him and it wasn't going to leave any part of him untouched. All that burning and burning—

Out of the mist there was a face he had never seen before, a man with black eyes behind round spectacles; his lips were moving and his hands unseen were doing something to the pain below. Before the mist covered it all he thought he saw Isabella's face. But that must have been the pain because Isabella could have no part in this—she belonged to life, another life, years and years ago.

He was remembering a line of poetry from a long way past, about "the years and the months which are the rags of time." He would never know anything because his time had stopped, the sequence broken.

Over and over he was living the same dream, and the focal point was Luis Mundaya in a beam of light, staggering and spreading his arms out, twirling round with his white hair flying, and then disappearing into the light.

The man with the dark eyes and the round spectacles was there again and this time there wasn't any mist. He was very nearly a bald man and he was smiling.

" Well, Mr. Conn-ell, and how do you feel now?"

It was a soft voice, precise, breaking his name into two distinct syllables and getting the accent at the end.

Charles was trying to move and the man's hand was firm on his shoulder.

" Be still, Mr. Conn-ell. You must not try to move yourself yet. I am your doctor and you must do as I tell you and soon we will have you very well again— Hear me?"

It was no good. Even his head wasn't going to obey him. It was odd to feel so utterly tired and weak.

There was a firm hand at the back of his neck lifting him gently, and the cool rim of a glass against his mouth. And then more quiet enveloping sleep and more faint faces floating over him : the man in the spectacles—and Isabella, smiling this time and really being there. Sleep.

It was dark when he woke and the pain in his side had become strictly local; he could feel his arms and fingers; and the thick swath of bandaging across his middle. He was even able to rub his hand over his jaw and hear the rasp of the beard. This was really himself and by God did he need a shave.

There was a little soft light there at the foot of the bed among the shadows. A large dark dress and a heavy face, eyes watching him, knitting needles flashing. Eulalia.

Without a sound she was beside him, smiling, large and friendly.

" Hullo," he said. " Is it night?"

Her hand on his forehead was very gentle.

" *Pobrecito*."

He closed his eyes. Poor little one. And that was precisely how he felt.

Later Isabella was there, sitting and holding his hand, whispering to him not to try to talk and not to move but just rest still. She was smiling but when she lifted his hand to her lips he saw the tears and turned his head towards her. But he couldn't say anything—the last thing he remembered was her lips on his forehead and the gentle brush of her hair against his cheek. Then he really knew that he was alive.

Daylight and bright sunshine filled the small room; a sad Madonna watched from the wall by the door.

There were pillows at his back. Isabella sat with her hands folded in her lap, very still and erect in a black frock; there had been no emotion in her voice as she told him about her father.

" He was buried yesterday."

" I'm sorry, darling . . ."

" It was the shock and the exertion. He wasn't wounded, Charles, not like you. He just died."

" I think I knew it, when we got to the tunnel . . . José was quite heroic."

She smiled. " He doesn't think you're too bad either."

" I didn't do a thing but get in the way of a bullet. I was a dead loss when the emergency came. José was the one . . . he did it all . . . I still don't understand how I got back here—all I can remember is fainting in the tunnel. That was José again, I suppose?"

" And Guillermo. José carried my father here. Then he went for Guillermo and they took a sheep hurdle and some rope. It must have been a dreadful journey for you, darling. You'd lost so much blood by then."

He shook his head. " Didn't know a thing . . . not after being in the tunnel . . . I can remember shouting for Harry."

" José would have killed him if he had found him. He

left after the shooting. He didn't even come back to pick up anything from your camp. He just went. I waited all night, expecting him, but with my father and then you it didn't seem to matter what Harry did."

Charles closed his eyes. "I'm sorry, darling, it was my fault. I should never have brought him."

She took his hand. "Darling, you're being silly. None of it was your fault."

"Damn Harry Warrender!" he said. "Damn and blast Harry Warrender to hell! I would never have believed it—"

"He saw his chance," she said, "and he took it. Perhaps he was frightened. José says the two of them were just coming into the courtyard when it started. José couldn't understand why you and my father were so long. They had the pictures in the car and they were ready to leave. So they came back up for you. Then the shooting started—and José didn't see Harry Warrender after that."

"He probably thought none of us would come out of it alive—and he had a gun himself. The swine—all the way along you didn't like him, and how right you were!"

"If you excite yourself any more I'll leave you and send Eulalia in." She tucked his hand back inside the bed-clothes briskly, smiling. The black dress made her look very slender and young.

"I'm sorry about your father," he whispered. "More sorry than I can say—it needn't have happened. It was only because he was so anxious to show me the house and they caught us in the hall and we had to run."

"They left early the next morning," Isabella said flatly. "Ludmilla Carceres and her lover: I had great trouble keeping José here that night; he wanted to go back and kill the man, and if there had been any wound on my

father I don't think anything in the world would have
stopped José, and even now I wouldn't give much for that
young man's life if José ever met him."

"The shooting was quite deliberate," Charles said.
"When he got us in the light of his torch outside he was
laughing."

"They left together in a hurry in her car. Ludmilla
must have recognised my father. Nothing was reported to
the police, but I imagine the two servants in the house
must have heard something; at all events the *Guardia
Civil* were here on Sunday, asking questions; fortunately
Doctor Abacero from Molledo was here; he has been looking after my father, and you as well. He trained in London
and everyone knows him as the best doctor around here.
He told them my father's death was from natural causes
and he didn't say anything about you, up here in bed. If
they had any suspicions there wasn't anything they could
do—Ludmilla Carceres hadn't made any report of an
attempted burglary. Guillermo removed your tents and
equipment, and as far as the *Guardia Civil* are concerned
the two English campers have just moved on as un-
expectedly as they came."

"That's true of one of them at least," said Charles.
"And there's been no word at all from Harry of course?"

"He's in France," she said. "I had a cable sent to
Joachim Menendez from Santander. That was on Saturday, the day after all this happened; I told him the paintings had gone astray and asked him not to buy them if
they were offered to him. His reply came yesterday afternoon: Harry Warrender had been on the phone to him
from Paris and he wanted Menendez to meet him there;
he said he had a letter from my father and that he was
acting for my father. He had the paintings by Zurbaran."

Isabella got up and went over to look out of the small window. " I'm not terribly concerned about those paintings —they aren't worth what they cost my father, and you— but I'd hate to think of Harry Warrender getting away with this so easily. My father is in his grave, and you've had a bullet through your side, and Harry Warrender is in Paris hoping to collect the money."

" The question is how badly does Menendez want the pictures? Is he going to Paris?"

" Not yet," said Isabella. " He had my cable before Harry Warrender rang so he wasn't really surprised at the offer—not as surprised as Warrender thought he might be. Joachim is no fool: he didn't make his millions by not having all his wits about him, so he put Warrender off and said he had arranged to spend a few days in Ireland look- ing at some horses; he owns a bloodstock stud amongst other things. Warrender is to contact him again at the end of the week. Warrender didn't give him any address. Menendez wants the pictures but he knows something is wrong."

" Harry's taking a chance," said Charles thoughtfully. " He'd expect you to get in touch with Menendez some- time, and what he's gambling on is Joachim's supposed willingness to get the pictures by whatever means he can. Harry's a little out of his depth and he hasn't got another prospective customer lined up yet—he badly needs an un- scrupulous rich collector and he hopes Menendez is it. So we've got until the end of the week."

" We?" Isabella smiled as she came back. " Darling, you're not going to be able to move from that bed for at least another week. You've been a very sick man."

" I feel fine," he said. " I'd like a shave. Tomorrow, perhaps, I could walk—"

" Not you." Gently she eased him back against his pillows. " I'll bring you some hot water and shaving things, and afterwards you must sleep until Doctor Abacero sees you this afternoon. Now promise you'll be good and lie there and not do anything silly, your side is mending very nicely."

It was better after he had shaved. He tried a cigarette but it made him giddy; Eulalia's chicken soup was a much better attraction.

Later, at lunch time when the blinds were drawn against the sun, José came up to see him, tip-toeing in and plainly delighted not to find him moribund; they enjoyed an interesting exchange of vocabularies, so much so that before he left José could manage " Good show, chaps " very creditably; he also dredged up " lousy bastard " from recollections of earlier cultural contacts with the seamen who put in to Bilbao, and both of them knew to whom he referred.

Doctor Abacero turned out to be a plump smiling little man in an English tweed jacket, not very new but still very good. He was deft and cheerful and quite incurious as to how this stray Englishman had come to have a bullet bouncing off one of his lower ribs.

He changed the dressing and said : " You are a lucky young man. You will be a little stiff for some days yet and you will be doing positively no jumping about. You are hearing me, Mr. Conn-ell?"

" Thanks, Doctor. How soon can I leave?" said Charles.

Doctor Abacero looked at Isabella's smiling face and said :

" When I was a student at St. Mary's Hospital in Paddington I heard much of the Englishman's lack of gallantry : this is the best evidence of it I have ever seen,

Señorita Isabella. He cannot leave you fast enough. You and the good Eulalia wait on him hand and foot, and what is his first question?"

"You've got it all wrong," said Charles. "When I leave she's coming with me."

The doctor's eyes gleamed behind his round spectacles and he showed tiny white even teeth.

"Such outrageous good fortune for you, young man. I understand why your temperature does not behave. My congratulations to you both."

"Thanks," said Charles. "Now when can I get up?"

"Friday, perhaps. Now, Señorita Isabella, you wish to use my telephone. Let us go and leave the worthless young man to his dreams. Mr. Conn-ell, if you put your foot outside that bed before Friday morning I will inform the *Guardia Civil* that you are an international dealer in drugs and that you carry a Communist Party membership card. Also that I believe it is your intention to kidnap Señorita Isabella Mundaya for an unchivalrous purpose that will be a disgrace to the fair name of *España*. And so on. And so on. I bid you *buenas tardes,* Mr. Conn-ell!"

Charles grinned. The doctor took Isabella's arm with much ceremony; his good English tweed jacket was a little tight for him and his rear view was distinctly plump.

Over her shoulder Isabella was smiling her helpless confusion.

"I have to go with him," she said. "He has the only available telephone in these parts and I must talk to Menendez. Be very good, darling, please."

"I haven't any choice," Charles said. "Hurry back."

13

IT WAS almost dark before she returned; he had been dozing and watching the shadows creep across the room; there was very little furniture, some heavy old dark pieces that had seen generations of wear; on a high square chest of drawers there were two faded photographs in plain frames; a young woman with a baby on her lap, the other was of a group of smiling young men in short scholars' gowns and he thought he could recognise his father's face among them.

So he was in Luis Mundaya's room. There couldn't be any spare accommodation in the farmhouse: Isabella and Eulalia and Luis Mundaya—that must have been the limit of the upstairs rooms; and José had to sleep somewhere.

Yesterday they had buried Luis Mundaya and he should have been there with Isabella—he shifted impatiently and the quick tug of pain in his side reminded him of his continuing disability. If only he had been quicker that bullet would never have got him—José had charged right up to that murderous fool with a gun and José hadn't been damaged. Thinking of Harry Warrender didn't make him feel any better—he could hear Harry stating his belief that you always had to look after Number One, and that was exactly what Harry Warrender had done.

It was really frightening to think how a long friendship of some twenty odd years had been snapped completely by greed and cowardice and lack of good faith. And now Harry was in Paris preparing to sell the paintings to Menendez—or to anyone else who had the money and wouldn't ask questions; there would be dishonest dealers in Paris and if he hung around long enough Harry would find one—he had a nose for that kind of man.

Isabella looked tired. "Menendez was out," she said. "I tried the Dorchester first and his secretary tried to locate him for me and get him to a phone. It was such a business, holding on and holding on and being passed from one to the other. I got him in the end, though, and I told him everything, darling—my father, and you, and what Harry Warrender had done. He was more than sympathetic. When Warrender rings him he's going to coax him into coming to London and pretend it's because of the currency regulations—I'm sure he can make it sound convincing— he did to me. He'll admit to Warrender that he has heard from me but he'll pretend it doesn't make very much difference to him : he wants the pictures so badly that he doesn't care how he gets them. He says he can make Harry Warrender believe they are just a pair of sharp boys fixing a deal. And I'm confident he can."

"I want to be in London when this happens. I must. Menendez can have his pictures—all I want is Harry." Charles tried to sit up straight against his pillows and met with little success.

Isabella eased him back. Very gently she said : "Darling, you won't be in any state for fighting for a long time —and I'm glad—there's been enough violence."

Charles scowled at himself. "But we've got to fix Harry Warrender. I can't just lie here and let him help himself to what belongs to you."

She smiled. " I don't think I care about that very much now. Nothing we can do will ever stop Harry Warrender being a crook. And there's another thing, darling: when you were hurt I sent a cable to your father. I had to tell him and I was really terribly worried about you. I just told him you'd had an accident. I spoke to him from Doctor Abacero's this afternoon. And I told him most of it. I had to, darling—cables and air-mail letters weren't really any use and you'd been unconscious and feverish for so long. He's arranging an air passage and he'll be here on Friday—I told him you were doing well now but I didn't try to stop him."

She folded the sheet neatly across Charles's chest. He moved his right arm, round her neck, and there was no resistance. Her hair slid over his face in a sweet scented mesh and her mouth was warm, soft and infinitely tender.

" The best tonic in the world," he murmured. " I believe I'm going to enjoy this convalescence." He stroked her neck lingeringly; her chin fitted into the cup of his hand and she was kneeling by his bed.

" I've been so frightened," she whispered. " First my father—José bringing him back to me like that and I'd been waiting hours and hours—and then you, darling." She rested her head against his shoulder, holding him, hiding herself.

" All that's over now," he said quietly, stroking her hair, " you mustn't think of it any more, my darling—we'll all go back with my father, next week, as soon as we can. I feel better every minute—"

She wept a little, quietly; and for long silent minutes she was unmoving against him, while he kissed her fingers one by one and the delicate soft inside of her wrist and he was wondering how ever he had endured his life before without this; how pitifully incomplete he had been, and he had never known.

She remained with him until he slept and it was the sweetest sliding into sleep that he could ever remember, because the last thing he saw was the smiling of her lips in the lamplight, and the last thing he heard was her soft whispered : " Good night, darling, sleep well."

By Thursday evening he had privately defied Doctor Abacero's edict while Isabella was below getting his supper tray ready. He was able to stand by his bed and totter a few steps, first to the chest of drawers, and then as far as the window; he shuffled around in his bare feet on the dark polished boards; his legs were uncertain and liable to give at the knee without warning, and under the bandage round his middle the pain had become an exasperating itch; earlier that afternoon Doctor Abacero had said it was all doing beautifully and that he expected the patient to live.

The thin cotton pyjamas had almost no colour left in them, and the legs were rather too short for him; they must have belonged to Luis Mundaya; on the pocket he could just pick out the faded outline where the initials " L.M." had once been embroidered; he noticed that the photographs from the chest had gone, and all in an instant he found himself consumed with an urgency to get her away from there, back to London, Weybridge—a house where there would be no reminders—where she could live with him and let him show her how she was cherished and loved for as long as the breath was in him. He promised himself he was going to do everything to help her to forget that appalling night when José had carried back to her the lifeless body of her father.

The next day, feeling rather fraudulent, he demonstrated the extent of his recovery to Doctor Abacero and was allowed to put on trousers and a shirt and he helped downstairs to sit in the sun; the household fussed about him and it was very pleasant. In one short week so much had happened; he found himself waiting for the thin figure of Luis Mundaya to appear with the wild white hair and the hunched shoulder and the quiet pleasant voice—and it must be so much worse for Isabella; everything about the farm would remind her of her father.

Guillermo brought Chico to talk to him, and Guillermo himself waved aside any thanks for his part in helping to get the Señor back: his regret was that he hadn't been with them in the first place because then he assured Charles, it would have been very different, by God it would!

There could be no question of offering money to men like José and Guillermo; he had talked about it with Isabella and she said he couldn't offer them a greater insult. To Guillermo he suggested that Chico might like to keep the tents and camping equipment, including the primus, and Chico for a few moments was ecstatic at the thought of what this would do to his prestige among his associates in the village.

There was no sign of Connell Senior; later in the evening a youth arrived on a bicycle with a message from Doctor Abacero; Isabella had given the doctor's number to Charles's father. Connell Senior was in a hotel at Santander; he had flown by B.E.A. to Biarritz, then on the airline coach to San Sebastian where he had hired a car; he would wait to hear from them in the morning and suggested he would like a guide.

In the early morning Isabella walked down into the valley and beyond the village to catch the country bus into Santander, and remembering the long-established eccentricities of his father's driving Charles advised her to make sure she took the wheel before they got to the real country roads.

"I look forward to hearing his version of how he got from San Sebastian to Santander, especially in a strange car. He doesn't drive a car," said Charles, "he fights with it. It's a battle. And he never has an accident, oddly enough."

"He's a pet," said Isabella, "coming all that way. I'll be very tactful with him."

It was lunch time before a black Ford Consul with a left-hand drive crawled up the track to the farm, and Isabella was driving. Her passenger got out, straightened his light-weight grey jacket, and gave a half-salute to Charles before walking briskly over with Isabella.

John Connell looked exactly what he was: a semi-retired professional man with an excellent digestion, no financial worries, and the placid settled habit of mind that might be expected to follow from such a pleasant and fortunate combination; traditionally conservative in his tastes, balanced in his judgments, and mentally alert, he still found life satisfying and reasonable. On the drive back Isabella had discovered herself thinking what an excellent grandfather he would be, which would have delighted him enormously if he had been able to guess at her line of thought, unmaidenly and premature thought it most certainly was.

I

" Well, Charles," said John Connell cheerfully, " I hear the most extraordinary things about you from Isabella."

" It hasn't exactly been a howling success, I'm afraid."

" You should have told me, Charles."

" I didn't want to worry you."

" Huh," said John Connell. " A likely story. What am I, a neurotic ?"

" You're splendid," said Charles. " That was quite a journey you had for yourself yesterday. Aeroplane trips and everything."

" You're too big for me to beat," said John Connell, " but there used to be a time, my son, when I'd take the hide off you for an impertinence like that."

Charles smiled at Isabella. " He's a dear old thing, really. Used to design hen coops and dog kennels. You mightn't believe it, but he's still got some of his faculties."

" Lunch," said Isabella. " You can fight afterwards." She had never had a brother; there was something comforting and sane in the way Charles and his father fitted each other so easily and without question.

Lightheartedly they exchanged near-insults throughout lunch and John Connell retailed some picturesque and colourful details of his son's boyhood, and Isabella was surprised to find herself laughing at the major improbabilities that grew as John Connell got into his stride, in spite of Charles's vehement denials; this was the way it ought always to be, she was thinking, with a family—no heartache or tragic loss.

They argued amicably about Harry Warrender.

" Never liked the feller," said John Connell, " even when you were kids together, Charles. There was a basic weakness in him somewhere. Terribly polite and charming when he felt like it, but it didn't *mean* anything."

" I blame myself for bringing him here," said Charles, " it was my idea."

" That's nonsense," Isabella said warmly, " now you'll make me angry if you go on saying that !"

" Harry knew what he was doing," said John Connell. " If there had been no trouble when you got those paintings I think Harry Warrender would have betrayed himself. It was the emergency that was too much for him. Like the time they kicked him out of the Army. When do you expect to be fit to travel, Charles ?"

Charles got up and walked carefully round the table to prove his mobility. " Ready to go anywhere," he said.

John Connell inspected him. " And this is the disrespectful whelp who makes disparaging remarks about my faculties. Make him sit down, Isabella, before he collapses at my feet."

" On Monday," said Charles. " Monday at the latest. I never felt better. And there are things to be done in London."

Later that afternoon Isabella took John Connell down to the churchyard behind the untidy cypresses that surrounded the old church. It was so quiet and still in the hot sun and Isabella knelt by the newly-turned grave with bright flowers cradled in her arms, and John Connell found himself on his knees for the first time for too many years.

And when they turned away her hand was light on his arm and he could not make himself look at her because a man of his age ought not to have tears in his eyes in front of a girl who has just left her father's grave and who walks with her head so proudly held and all that quiet courage in her heart.

It was a long way back to those Cambridge days. An old friend, a very old and dear friend—the best.

"When you go," she said softly, "you and Charles— may I come with you, please?"

"Of course," he said, "of course."

"Sometime," she said in a small reflective voice, "some-time I want to come back here. I will always want to come back here, I think—will Charles mind?"

He tucked her hand under his arm and that was answer enough for her.

"We've been very lucky," she said, "Charles and I. In the fathers we've had, I mean."

John Connell cleared his throat awkwardly.

"Now that's the nicest thing anyone has said to me for as long as I can remember."

"I mean it," she said with a sudden intensity. "Charles and I want to get married, Mr. Connell—my father knew about it—he liked Charles and he knew how much we love each other—and he told me he was glad—"

He met her earnest gaze and he smiled slowly. "Luis and I never disagreed seriously about anything that mattered—I remember, we argued about the things that weren't essential. You know, Isabella, long ago your father and I used to talk about this happening, you and Charles : you were just a baby then, but we used to plan it all—so it makes me very happy to see it coming true : I could just have wished that the circumstances had been different— then your father and I would have been two very, very happy, men, my dear."

He paused for a moment. Then went on, in a quieter voice : "I'm glad you let me come with you this afternoon —and for whatever else must be done here you must let it be my privilege as an old friend."

She could say nothing. They had come out of the darkness of the lined cypresses into the radiance of the late afternoon sun.

" Charles will bring you back here whenever you wish," said John Connell. " You have my promise for that."

That night John Connell drove back to his hotel in Santander, and before he returned the next day he showed considerable energy in getting air passages back to London for all three of them; Wednesday was the earliest it could be arranged, and he agreed with Isabella that the longer Charles remained convalescent the better.

Early on Tuesday morning they set out for San Sebastian. Eulalia wept volcanically and found no comfort in any reassurances that Señorita Isabella would be back to visit them all; after some difficulty Charles had persuaded José to accept his wrist watch as a token of his esteem, and it had taken some very tactful negotiating with José very much on his dignity for a while and full of pride : Señor Luis had been his *patron* and it had been an honour to serve him—the Señor's *reloj* was very fine and José would always carry it in memory of their friendship. It was quite a ceremony.

Isabella used her charm and coaxed John Connell into letting her drive and she was glad to have something to occupy her during those first few minutes when they bumped slowly down the farm track and turned into the road. Part of her life had ended back there; what had begun as an adventure, unorthodox and lighthearted perhaps, had finished so very differently—even Harry Warrender could never be the same man again.

She drove very carefully with Charles on the back seat and John Connell beside her. They were in San Sebastian by the early evening, and although Charles maintained he felt perfectly fine his face gave him away and after a light supper they got him to bed in the hotel with one of Doctor Abacero's sleeping pills.

Isabella's ticket had been a London to Madrid return but John Connell had arranged an exchange for her for the return by Biarritz, and the next morning they were on the airline coach; at Irun Charles thought about Harry Warrender bringing the Humber back with its precious and unsuspected cargo after driving all through the night; it was difficult to imagine what might be in the mind of a man you thought you knew, at a time like that—panic, relief—no touch of conscience—? How long had this been in Harry's mind? And was that why he had brought a gun? Just in case the opportunity came for a large profit?

Harry had been anything but prosperous; shady, clinging to a way of life that had evidently become more precarious each year. But what he had done to them back there in Spain, that had been something of another order. Vicious, criminal—that was Harry Warrender now. And after all those years when he'd been telling himself he liked old Harry in spite of everything—good fun, amusing to be with, didn't give a damn for anybody, and all that. Now he was a crook.

PART THREE

—AND BACK AGAIN

14

THE TWO small boys bumped on their bicycles into the clearing, whooping and swinging their feet clear of the pedals as they tried to ride down the ruts. It was much more interesting than riding on the road and the one who fell off first was a pig with red ears and fleas.

In the clearing they circled slowly round and this time they were Billy Smart's Circus; the bare-backed rider fell off his saddle and scraped his knee on a pedal and swore the way he had heard his father, and that made them both giggle.

So they sat under a tree and tossed who ought to have the odd ham roll of the five they'd bought; they smoked a cigarette each with much nonchalance, leaning elegantly on their elbows and tapping the ash on to the grass long before it had any chance to form.

The rusty old water tank over there by the busted-down wall asked for attention. Nothing in the world is so satisfying as the *clunk* of a brick against a rusty old empty tank. Nearly as good as busting a window. Better, really, because you didn't have to bolt for your life afterwards and get a walloping from your old man.

Ammunition was plentiful and exhilaration grew as the target boomed and boomed under the barrage. One of them laid odds of fifty million quid to any sum his partner cared to raise that he'd bust a brick clean through that old tank before they finished.

The angry swarming of the flies over the tank suspended operations. There was a whole cloud of them, whizzing about like mad, flies, blue bottles, all sorts.

"Hey, bet there's something inside that old tank. Let's look. You give us a bunk-up, Reg."

Reg was willing, though he remarked that it didn't half stink as they got near the tank.

"Golly," agreed his companion, George, "you said it. Must be some old rat or a rabbit maybe."

"Talk sense," said Reg, stooping. "It's got that wooden lid on the top. Like to see a rabbit shift that, old cock. Don't be daft."

George giggled and waved his cap at the swarming flies and he was suddenly sorry he suggested looking first. He climbed gingerly up, pushed at the edge of the wooden cover and looked down into the opening. For just one second.

Then he fell off his companion's back, knelt with his hand over his mouth.

"What's the matter with you?" said Reg.

George spewed on the grass. The flies buzzed noisily and angrily over the tank and inside the tank and all around the opening. And the smell—

Reg swallowed his nausea and ducked away. George was crawling over the grass and he hadn't got anything left to be sick on. His face was yellow and his eyes were running but you could tell he wasn't blubbing.

They faced each other in the clearing. Reg stole a careful look back at the tank.

"What was it? You see something?"

George wiped his mouth on the sleeve of his jersey.

" I dunno. I think it was a body—I didn't really look —see for yourself if you don't believe me."

" No fear— I never smelt such a stink. Hey, George, you suppose we found a body, a dead body? Murdered or something? Gosh, we'll be pretty famous, won't we?"

George had recovered; he felt weak and by no means full of the spirit of adventure.

" I know what my old man will do to me," he said with the conviction of long experience. " He'll warm my back-side. We're supposed to be at choir practice."

" Ruddy old choir practice," said Reg. " Let's get our bikes and tell the bobbie."

" You can tell him and see how you like being famous. Golly, you didn't see what I saw, Reg—it was awful!"

They rode down the track a good deal faster than they had come. Two very frightened and perspiring young despatch riders who ought to have been at choir practice and who now regretted the omission, and within an hour the old brickyard under the trees was full of activity, with screens and photographers and an ambulance and at least three police cars. And George might have been relieved to know that his stomach wasn't the only one to rebel at what was brought out of that rusty old tank.

The three motor cyclists in a light arrow formation spurted up the road, swerved into the kerb, slipped into a line with barely a yard interval between machines, and stopped. All three riders wore identical outfits: black jackets of shiny leather; tightly belted and zip-fastened up to the chin, tight black trousers and buckled suède boots.

The front rider put his machine up on its strut. He was the tallest of the three, black-haired with a brooding bad-tempered face. He peeled off his gauntlets and looked at the shabby front of the house without any show of interest.

"See you," he said to his two companions, and then walked stiff legged up the steps and into the house, slapping the gauntlets against his thigh.

Straddling their machines his companions lit cigarettes and watched the first floor windows; they looked like twin brothers: long sandy hair and heavy faces with underslung jaws, grey eyes with almost no colour at all. A girl in a light red dress came down the pavement. They watched her, saying not a word, rigid, immobile, drilled. The two heads moved, following her. She might have been naked. She passed them, head high, fidgeting with herself. There was no sound but the *tock-tock-tock* of her sharp heels.

As precisely and uniformly as two guardsmen on parade they turned from the waist up, still straddling their machines. She was still well within hearing.

One of them said just a single four-letter word, flatly, loudly, deliberately.

The girl's head jerked; she half looked over her shoulder, and hurried on, her head lowered.

The two riders exchanged a brief glance. The one who had spoken lifted one shoulder and said. "She knew it. That makes it a quid you owe me."

"You go to hell," said the other. "She was on her own and that only counts half. What about the one I give it to in the caff? With her mum? You owe me ten, cocker, and don't you forget."

The woman in the apron was tired; behind her the radio blared. She didn't like the look of the young loafer in the leather jacket or the way he put his questions.

"If he's gorn I know nothing about it and he never said a word to me. Rent's paid up for another week. I'll start worrying then. Anyway, how do you know he's gorn?"

"How would I know, ma? I looked. He took his clothes."

"You looked? Well I like your ruddy sauce, young feller! How'd you get in, if I might ask?"

The young man took a key out of his pocket and stuffed it into a pocket of her apron. "Don't get yourself all heated up, ma, I just looked."

"The nerve of it! The ruddy nerve! Snooping round my apartments while my tenant is out!"

The young man was leaning against the door. "Have to find yourself a new tenant for those rooms, ma. Warrender won't be around to pay you your rent. You haven't seen him since Sunday, right?"

"I run a perfectly respectable house here, I'd have you know. And don't you call me ma, you lippy young basket you!"

The young man planted his hand flat on the woman's fat flushed face and pushed. He slammed the door on her shrill screaming, strode through the dim hall and out to the steps, drawing on his gauntlets. His two outriders kicked their engines into life and opened their throttles.

In that tight-arrow formation they surged down the road and their combined acceleration was a contemptuous crescendo, window-rattling like bomb blast. Behind them in the house the landlady gave herself a stiff neat gin to recover her dignity, then she waddled up the stairs and inspected Harry Warrender's rooms. He'd left all right, she knew the signs; him and that brassy-haired trollop of his; hopefully she searched but there wasn't a drop of stuff left in the place, and the bed not even made. Must have gone Sunday afternoon when she was resting her feet. No letters for him. There never were. Mister Harry-Bloody-Warrender. She'd put a card in the sweet shop down the corner, and this time she'd ask to see their marriage lines. Fun was fun and nobody could ever accuse her of not being broad-minded, but a married couple with the hubbie in regular work was what you wanted. No kids of course. Make a place messy, running up and down the stairs and blocking the lavatory. She found a packet of cigarettes in a table drawer and lit up as she finished her inspection.

In a cheap fibre suitcase stuck on top of the wardrobe she found some packets of photographs that proved what she'd always thought about her former lodger's interests— that blonde tart hadn't been the first he'd had up there.

She locked the rooms and went downstairs. If that saucy young feller in the fancy jacket ever showed his face again she'd give him the flat of her frying pan, by God she would.

The young man and his two lieutenants continued their pilgrimage, indefatigably, patiently and with an intelligent co-ordination that would have surprised their parents or occasional employers or any of the others who looked upon them as a bunch of shiftless loafers without half a real brain between them; there were plenty of offers of help from young men who would be glad to be accepted by the trio even as junior acolytes; but these three were the élite; their accomplishments were whispered over; nobody ever *proved* anything, not even the police.

They spent some time in a café with a dressy young man who owned a cream Ford Prefect and worked for a music publisher. Sure he'd been out with Sandra and what of it? No, he didn't know where she was and he'd never heard of a bloke named Warrender and they could take it or leave it. Tough and independent. At first.

The tallest of the three had been doing the questioning.

He slid the café table forward so that its sharp edge pinned the dressy young man by the chest against the wall and for the first time he was beginning to see that there might be reason to be frightened. The one with the black hair was Sandra's brother Tommy and he'd heard about him, oh yes, he'd heard all right.

Holding the table in place Tommy looked at the two on his flanks also holding the table.

" Three against one," he said. " We get no sense of fair play. Ought to be ashamed of ourselves."

Nobody else in the coffee bar was taking any notice of them : four young men in earnest conference over cups of coffee; quiet thoughtful types.

" Honest to God I haven't seen her since Friday week !"

" Saturday night, son, Saturday night—that's what I want to hear." Tommy's whisper was very penetrating.

" I swear she wasn't with me and that's the God's truth ! I can prove it—I was with my boss over at Golders Green, you ask him, he'll tell you—move that table—I can't breathe !"

Tommy unscrewed the top of the wooden pepper pot very slowly.

" True or false ?" he said softly.

The young man shook his head; the narrow lapels of his striped Italian style jacket were pushed up about his neck and his face was very damp; he couldn't see anything but that pepper pot, tilted towards him in Tommy's fingers. The three of them were waiting for him, Tommy talking.

" Tell me about Harry Warrender."

" I've never heard of him. Honest to God I never did— I don't know anyone of that name !" The young man swallowed and he knew it was no good telling himself he wasn't as scared as all hell. That Tommy—he could think of the pepper streaming into his eyes—just a flick of the wrist only a few inches away from his face.

"Tommy," he whispered, " I'd tell you if I knew him I'd tell you—God I would—you *know* I would!"

Tommy looked at his companions and pursed his lips. They said nothing. Just waiting for the word from Tommy.

" Please—" the young man whispered, " you got nothing against me, Tommy—I haven't seen Sandra since that Friday and I don't know this Warrender bloke—that's the gospel truth—" He shook his head. The edge of the table was cutting into his chest.

Tommy replaced the top of the pepper pot, twisting his strong stubby fingers very slowly and not looking at what he was doing, and the relief on the young man's face was instant and he tried to smile ingratiatingly to prove his total lack of ill-will.

" Anything I can do, Tommy," he said eagerly. " I'll ask about this bloke—what's he look like, Tommy?"

Tommy stretched forward and slapped him across the cheek, lightly, slowly, using his fingers only.

" Button it, son," said Tommy. He stood up and his two companions followed him out and in the crowded café people got out of their way without being invited.

The cream Ford Prefect stood by the kerb; their motor cycles waited in the side road; one of them took out a knife and casually ran his hand along the car leaving a deep mark cutting into the metal, like a small boy chalking on a fence; just as casually he walked round the other side of the car and repeated the damage; squatting by each wheel in turn he slashed the walls of the tyres, whistling softly to himself. Then he joined the other two and they continued the search.

Striker Lewis was unlucky, considering how discreetly he

had managed his affairs for so many years. They met some-body who remembered seeing Warrender and Striker Lewis in a pub not so long ago and Warrender had been buying the drinks.

They caught Striker in his little office and when he mistakenly and unwisely reached for the telephone Tommy broke his spectacles and pushed him around the floor with his boot. So Striker became co-operative and told them about the Humber; he had some trouble convincing Tommy that he hadn't seen Harry Warrender since the job had been completed—it had been a straight business trans-action and paid for on the nail.

" Lives over Kilburn way," he said, " but I swear to you gents I couldn't tell you where; he just paid for the job and off he went and if I'd known there was gonna be this fuss you got my oath for it I'd have seen the twister further before I let him into my shop."

Tommy shook Striker backwards and forwards and they left him in the débris of his office groping blindly around for his shattered spectacles.

The first notice in the newspaper just reported the find-ing of the body of a blonde girl in a disused water tank in the woods. Tommy missed that because he was no great reader. Later editions carried more interesting details con-cerning the find and a blurred picture of the water tank: " Scene of another sex murder?" Tommy took in the details. The girl had evidently been dead some days, and on the left leg of her knickers there was embroidered the name of Sandra.

Tommy got out of bed in a great hurry and for the first time in his short life he visited a police station of his own free will. And he went on his own.

K

15

THEY LANDED at London Airport in a depressing summer shower with the miles of tarmac gleaming in the wet, and After they had cleared the Customs the first thing Isabella did was ring Joachim Menendez at the Dorchester. He was out and she left a message that she would contact him in the evening. They took her home with them to Weybridge; John Connell insisted that she wasn't going to be left on her own in her small flat, not for the first few days at least, and she still had a few days of her holiday left. She hadn't needed much convincing : the thought of that quiet shaded house by the river with Charles was more attractive than she could say. The flat would be grim by herself.

" I had an odd phone call I forgot to mention," said John Connell. " It was the night before I left. It was a young man on the telephone and he wanted to know if I was Charles Connell. I told him I had a son by that name and then he said he wanted to talk to you, Charles. He wouldn't give me his name, but he sounded rather a rough type, I thought. A mixture of bogus American and cockney. I said you were abroad and I was fairly uppish about it. I told him I didn't care much for anonymous phone calls and he called me quite a rude name. Quite startling really.

So unexpected. I haven't been called one of those since I fouled a Welsh forward in a college match thirty odd years ago. But the really surprising part of it was that he asked me if you knew Harry Warrender and he was most anxious to find out when you were going to be home. I told him if it was all that important he could write to you and I'd see you got the letter in due course. So he called me another rude name and I put the phone down."

"Some of Harry Warrender's past catching up with him," said Charles. "I wonder how the anonymous young man linked me with Harry?"

"Somebody you met in one of Harry Warrender's pub expeditions," said his father. "Somebody Warrender owes money to, I'd suggest, from the tone of the young man's voice."

"There could be quite a queue of those," said Charles, "and none of them would sound very pleasant."

Early in the evening Isabella rang the Dorchester again and this time she was put through to Joachim Menendez in his suite, and he had interesting news: Harry Warrender had telephoned him the night before, not from Paris this time.

Joachim Menendez had a low rumbling voice that suggested he might be about to break into chesty laughter any minute; his English was careful but erratic.

"In London, I think he is, Miss Mundaya. And he begins to agitate with himself. Is frightened, I think, and I tell him the clever story: surely I will get him the money for those paintings. We are trusting one another, no?" Joachim laughed and it was like a barrel rolling over cobbles. "Like hell I am trusting him. I tell him I will meet him soon, tomorrow, the next day, what he wishes. And I have the money with me. You and I, we must talk of this,

Miss Mundaya and very soon. Arrangements we must make."

" We could come to you,'" Isabella suggested.

" Not good. Excuse. He knows you have told me about himself. Very nervous and frightened. Suppose he watched this hotel and you come to me? Too easily frightened. Better we meet elsewhere and talk. The Hotel at Paddington, perhaps? Nine o'clock?"

Charles said he was coming with her. This was something that concerned him.

" I brought Harry Warrender into it, and if there's any settling of accounts I'm going to be there, and I'd like to meet this Joachim Menendez—he sounds like a bright character, at least he has the good taste to be on our side."

Just before they left the phone rang. Charles answered it and recited the number politely.

" Charles Connell there?"

" I am Charles Connell. Who is that, please?"

" Never you mind. You a friend of Harry Warrender? You know him?"

"I do," said Charles. " Who are you?"

" You the bloke who gave him a cheque for three hundred quid?"

" I don't think I'm going to answer that," said Charles. " Why not give me your name? Or are you ashamed of it?"

" Never you mind, chum. Where's that bastard now?"

" Harry Warrender? Well now," said Charles, " I haven't the faintest idea. Who's lost him?"

" You're not being very smart. You been out on the fiddle with Harry Warrender. You give him three hundred quid. So all right. But where is he and don't tell me you don't know! I don't *like* it!"

"That covers both of us," said Charles. He put the phone down.

"More of the angry young man who wants Harry Warrender. Odd, he knew about the cheque I gave him."

The phone rang again, almost immediately. Charles let it ring. "We haven't time to fool around with any more of Harry Warrender's troubles. We've got enough."

The phone was ringing again as they left the house; John Connell had walked up the road for a game of snooker; the housekeeper was at the pictures; so the ill-mannered young man on the phone was going to be very angry indeed and it wasn't going to do him any good.

Joachin Menendez was in the Residents' Lounge, sitting on a small green upholstered settee; he had the quiet room all to himself except for a thin old clergyman brooding over a timetable in a corner and crossing and uncrossing his legs to show untidy grey socks.

Menendez wore a pearl-grey suit, a heavy cream silk shirt with a button-down collar and a deep bronze tie with a pearl pin; he had wide sloping shoulders and a long brown face; although he was nearly fifty his hair was thick and black; dark brown eyes, sharp and watchful and very intelligent, told you nothing of what he was thinking: they were the eyes of one who had schooled himself to wait and wait until the other man made the mistake. It was impossible to imagine Joachim Menendez ever taking a risk without having done everything to make sure that it wasn't going to be a risk after all. Then the power would show itself. In the hands of such a man as this Harry Warrender with his shiftiness and optimistic belief in his own shrewdness would be quite lost.

Joachim Menendez was wearing jewellery worth several thousands of pounds, but there was nothing effeminate about him.

Isabella introduced Charles, and Joachim asked polite questions about his injury and there was no denying his personal charm, effortlessly exercised and very real. He had the gift of making people feel important, and his unusual brand of English didn't seem to matter.

They would have something to drink? Of course. Isabella had gin and tonic, Joachim conferred with the waiter, found he was from Cyprus, moved easily into Greek, and got some brandy that even old and favoured clients seldom heard about.

It was abundantly clear Joachim Menendez enjoyed being a wealthy man; what he owned he had fought for himself, now he could buy what he wanted and he could see no reason for being ashamed of that.

" I think it will be tomorrow night," said Joachim Menendez. He spread his hands out in mid-air and balanced them up and down expressively. " I think in Paris he tried to sell, but that would be no easy thing, because there arrives a point when you must disclose what it is you have to sell or your client's interest and goodwill have left you. So you have three very valuable original paintings, masterpieces, and you fear to offer them for sale openly—you go to the clever boys in Paris, the sharp ones who will cut your throat and leave you with nothing." Joachim's smile didn't reach his eyes. " Paris frightened this Warrender. So back he is with me. I am a rogue. Naturally. I have no regard for the family of Mundaya. The paintings I want : what business of mine how they come to my hands? We are two clever rogues together."

"You're sure he doesn't suspect you?" Charles asked.
"He's not a fool."

"Money," said Menendez gently. "For some it sharpens
the brain, for others it blinds them—if we were talking
in hundreds this Warrender might be clever enough. But
we are talking in thousands. Thirty thousand pounds in
five-pound notes packed into a case and brought by me
when I receive the instructions." Menendez made a tent
of his fingers and blew through them. "It is too much for
this man to remain sensible over. All the time he is seeing
the money. And I am also a man of no honour, remember.
I am to remain in my hotel tomorrow at ten o'clock at
night and he is to telephone me. I have the money ready.
He believes that, have no fear he believes it."

"I wonder why he's waited so long," Charles said. "I
wonder why he hasn't tried to sell to you days ago—why
the delay?"

"He has a serious problem," said Joachim Menendez.
"He will not intend to stay in this country. No? You are
the friend he has betrayed so shamefully and you have now
come back, with Miss Mundaya whom he has robbed of the
last of her family's fortune. Correct? With thirty thousand
pounds the world is wide and can be made pleasant. The
difficulty is to take your money with you out of this country.
It is not impossible, but you must know the people who
will arrange it—I think Warrender has not been in a big
operation before, no?"

Charles Connell said : "I doubt it."

Joachim Menendez smiled very sadly and twisted the
ruby ring he wore on the middle finger of his left hand.

"What the Americans call it—out of his league, that
is our Warrender and he is finding that arrangements
expensive, I think, even if he has found the right people.

And yet he hasn't had the money: he is trying not to seem too anxious to deal with me, and I tell him I am a man of many many interests with much to occupy my time while I am in London. You understand? I tell him three paintings by Zurbaran are interesting and I will agree to buy them from him at the right figure if they reach me undamaged —but I have many claims on my time, I tell him, and thirty thousand pounds is not such a sum that I will lose my sleep for it—but I do not *give* it away."

" And tomorrow night?" said Isabella. " What happens then?"

" We meet," said Joachim. " Perhaps we talk more with each other. He will expect me to have the money with me, I think. I do not yet know where we meet but it will not be in a field under a haystack. I do not do business that way." He paused and added thoughtfully: " not now. If I am to buy those paintings tomorrow night, Miss Isabella, there will have to be a good light for me to see what I am getting, I must assure myself there has been no damage. I ask no questions how the pictures got from Spain and are here. It is not my business, but I will inspect them in a room with adequate light." He gave Isabella and Charles in turn a warm smile. " It would please me if you were there, it would be fitting and correct, I think."

" If you told us where," Charles said carefully, " we'd arrange to be there. Or at least I would."

Isabella chewed her lip and lowered her lashes. " Warrender has a gun," she said quietly. " Aren't you both forgetting that?"

" There was a gentleman in Caracas once," said Menendez. " He brought a gun to a friendly conference with me in a hotel bedroom. There was a question of money. And much anger." With one forefinger Menendez made a circle in the air. "No gun for Joachim. Not even a throwing knife. Now I am sitting here telling you and that one is is in his grave many years." He placed both clenched fists on the low table between them and smiled at Isabella. "I am older now, perhaps, and perhaps I have a little belly, but I have yet to meet the little crook who will take thirty thousand pounds from Joachim Menendez and live to be happy about it—"

Looking at him it didn't need much imagination to appreciate the force of his words.

"Now, Miss Isabella, we are understanding each other?"

Isabella smiled. "I think we do. I'm sure we do."

"Good. Very good. Tomorrow night, when I hear from you what it is Warrender proposes, then I will call you." Menendez shifted his gaze to Charles. "There will be no need for guns. You have been a sick man; Miss Isabella, she has told me of you: I am honoured to have your acquaintance. Tomorrow night we will use the clever brain against this Warrender. Together we will do it, and there is now nothing that I wish to do more than offer my assistance to Miss Isabella. Now shall we three drink to the misfortune of your former friend? And tomorrow night we will teach him that it is not a happy thing to betray a friend or steal from Luis Mundaya's daughter—"

Menendez rumbled internally for a moment and said: "Or to make a rogue out of Joachim Menendez who never steals from his friends!"

The elderly parson in the corner looked up deprecatingly at the amusement that was coming from that extraordinary-looking foreign gentleman with all that unsuitable jewellery, and it vaguely disturbed him to see that the nice English girl was joining in—or was she really English? One could never tell these days. But at least the young man was English, and that was a little reassuring.

"I have a last thought," said Joachim Menendez. "Warrender is by himself?"

Charles shook his head. "I frankly don't know. He knows a lot of people who aren't too particular about what they do. It didn't take him long to fix my father's Humber and that needed workshop facilities. You're wondering if he's picked up somebody to help him?"

"It may have been forced on him. I know he is agitating himself—it is in his voice even on the telephone."

"I couldn't even guess," said Charles. "But if I had to guess I'd say he was keeping this to himself—he wouldn't want to share the money."

"I will tell him," said Menendez abruptly. "I will tell him there must be nobody else tomorrow night or the deal finishes itself and I do not bring the money with me."

They left separately; Isabella and Charles went first and turned down the private way to the station to pick up Charles's car where they had left it by the arrival platforms; Charles found himself examining any men who bore even the remotest resemblance to Harry Warrender; it was quite absurd, of course; what was more worth thinking about was the possibility that Harry Warrender might have gone in with somebody else.

He wondered, and not for the first time since they'd heard that Warrender was in England, what would happen if they went to the police; whatever he and Isabella (and his father as well) thought about the paintings the official view would be that they belonged to Juan Carceres; they had been officially stolen, smuggled out of Spain and smuggled into this country. Isabella would have to be involved. He could imagine the office of the Director of Public Prosecutions getting the papers on the case and adding up the number of charges.

One day, when this was all over, he'd put the case purely hypothetically, to a barrister friend. But not now.

He was watching Isabella's profile as she drove up the station incline and turned into Praed Street. He was loving her frown of concentration.

"Darling," she said, "you're very quiet. What are you thinking of?"

"You," he said. "Where would you like to go for your honeymoon? Bermuda? Mexico? Florida? Nassau?"

It was a pleasant way to spend the time driving home. There was a long time together in front of them and all of it was going to be good and wonderful. Who could doubt it?

16

WHEN THEY reached the house in Weybridge they had still not settled the honeymoon, but they had moved on to the very satisfying topic of the kind of house Charles was going to design for them, and they had agreed that it was going to be a very special house indeed.

By the front door they saw a powerful motor-cycle squatting on its strut on the gravel and the lights were on in the sitting-room; the door was open as they came into the hall and they heard no sound of any conversation.

As they came into the sitting-room John Connell lowered his paper and said: "I came home to find we had company. Meet the eloquent young man of the telephone calls. The name is Tommy and he wants to see you, Charles. He has no conversational gifts that I can discover and he refuses to deal with me."

Tommy was in his usual uniform: shiny black leather jacket, tight black trousers and scuffed suède boots; he had his habitual sulky expression, read to turn to aggression and suspicion and who-the-hell-are-you-anyway; he was straddling a reversed chair much as he would straddle the saddle of his motor-cycle, the first two fingers of his right hand were yellow with nicotine, and he was smoking with an unbroken savagery as though he had a grudge against the cigarette and had to finish it as soon as possible.

He didn't get up as they came in and his scowl became just a little more pronounced.

" I been waiting," he said. Some dim recollection of past maternal tuition in the basics of manners prompted an awkward and surprising : " Evening, Miss."

He eyed Isabella expertly and openly. A judy with class. Wouldn't give you the time of day, not her. But class all right.

" Good evening," said Isabella pleasantly. " Sorry we kept you waiting."

" Well now," said Charles standing in front of Tommy, " our last conversation wasn't terribly cordial, as I remember it. But now that you're here, what can I do for you ?"

Tommy flicked his cigarette ash roughly in the direction of an ashtray.

" Harry Warrender," he said, " that's what you can do for me, mister."

" I told you," said Charles patiently, " I told you I don't know where he is. It would save you a lot of trouble if you believed me."

Tommy stared at him and rubbed one stubby hand along the top of his chair; one foot jigged up and down nervously; those who knew Tommy knew that when he began to fidget an unpleasant outburst was likely. Things got broken.

" I don't have to believe you. That's why I came down. So I'm here, mister, and I want a straight story. "

" You begin to annoy me," said Charles.

" Steady, Charles," said his father. " Shall I ring for the police and have him put out ?"

Tommy ignored John Connell and went on staring at Charles.

" Mister," he said, " you don't want any coppers—maybe you're not too bright and shiny yourself."

Isabella and Charles exchanged looks; they were both remembering what Joachim Menendez had suggested to them less than an hour ago: if Harry Warrender had any associates this Tommy might well be one of them and Warrender had done the dirty on him. Hence the search.

" Could tell a copper plenty myself," said Tommy. " All about that cheque for three hundred quid. You always sign your name in full, mister? It's a dead give away."

Charles sat down, and looked at their visitor with new interest. Tommy might possibly know more than it was comfortable for him to know, and the rest he might guess, if he was part of Harry Warrender's furtive circle. How much had Harry Warrender told him ?

" I know you been out of the country somewheres," said Tommy. " The old boy told me, and Harry Warrender was with you, right? Now you come back and I want to know where he is. I don't want any mess with you, mister. Just him."

" I can only repeat that I don't know where he is. We didn't come back together. But he's in England. That's all I can tell you."

" What was the three hundred for?"

Charles smiled. It would do no good to lose his temper. " If you can show me how it concerns you," he said as pleasantly as he could, " I might tell you."

" There's a smell, mister," said Tommy. " He had that cheque on the Friday and he cashed it on the Saturday and he beats it the next day. Out of the country. Right? You with him. Now you tell me what fiddle Harry Warrender was running with you."

Charles was hoping his relief wasn't showing in his face and he noticed Isabella's faint relaxing in her chair. Tommy didn't know anything that mattered.

" It must be the way your mind goes," said Charles, " or perhaps you knew Harry Warrender rather better than I did. Shall we say the money was the repayment of a loan?"

Tommy looked around the room; it wasn't all that smart but the house and grounds were well outside his normal range. His eyes shifted back to Charles.

"You never owed Harry Warrender any three hundred quid. Think I'm soft?"

"All right," said Charles, "I'm getting a little tired of this. Now why don't you get on that bike of yours and go back home? If you really know Warrender at all you'll know how he gets about—at this moment I don't know where he is. If you'd like to leave me your address I'll tell him—if I see him."

He stood up. Tommy didn't move at all; it was difficult to imagine what he might be thinking; that aggressive suspicious scowl seemed to be the normal front he presented to a hostile world.

"Perhaps," suggested Isabella slowly, "if we knew what was bothering you, why you wanted Warrender, we might be able to help. I can tell you this: he's no friend of ours."

Tommy examined her for a moment. He didn't understand that: it could be she was telling the truth, maybe both of them were.

He dug into the breast pocket of his leather jacket and took out a packet of cigarettes, offered it round perfunctorily and received no takers; he reached behind him and took out a flat wallet from the back pocket of his trousers; he unfolded a small newspaper cutting.

"You read the papers, mister?" He handed Charles the cutting. "You miss this one?"

Charles read it: 'Body of young woman found in disused water tank—police trying to identify her—developments expected.' His eye skimmed over the brief details.

Tommy tapped himself on the chest:

"I done the identification. My sister, that's who."

"I'm sorry," Charles said.

Tommy thrust his long thin legs out on each side of his chair. "You ever meet her? Her name was Sandra and she was a smart kid."

"No," said Charles slowly.

"Hope you're sure of that," said Tommy. "I been to the police. That was murder, mister. Her neck was broken. Just like that." He snapped his fingers. "She was drunk, they reckon, so she couldn't look after herself." He opened his mouth and let the cigarette smoke roll out as he spoke.

"I'm sorry," said Charles, "it must have been a dreadful shock for you and your family—but I'm quite certain I never met your sister."

"She was running around with Warrender. Five or six months. She was a good kid most .ways only she didn't pick her boy-friends right. I told her myself, I told her Warrender would give her the dirt and he did all right. Nobody seen her since the Saturday before last and I know she had a bust-up with him—she told me about it and she told me about that cheque you signed for Warrender, and the next day he beats it and nobody knows where he is. Nobody except maybe you, mister. And my sister's gone. And they find her in a tank with her neck busted. That mean anything to you?"

"If you're suggesting I know anything about your sister's death you're quite wrong," Charles said.

"So all right, but Warrender was a buddy of yours and the both of you leave the country same time as my sister disappears—and he's been getting money off you and you can't tell me it was on the level. Not with him—so the coppers might tie you up with this if they got round to you. You ever think of that?"

" You've told the police, of course?" said Isabella.

" They know Sandra and him had been together. Once I done the identifying for them." His mouth tightened. " I saw her the way she was when they found her." The back of the chair creaked under his grip and he whispered : " I just got to get that bloke, just me—"

" You'd better leave this to the police," said Charles. " It might not have been Warrender who killed your sister —she possibly had other men friends—"

" That's right, mister, but none of them disappeared. They're still around town."

" It could have been a stranger," Charles suggested.

" Aaah!" Tommy stubbed his cigarette out disgustedly on the heel of his boot and the sparks flew on the carpet. " You make me sick. Sticks out like Southend Pier : Warrender is the bloke I want and I want him before the coppers get him."

" I'm not defending Warrender," Charles said. " Don't think that, because I hate his guts. But you know this is mostly guesswork on your part—the only sensible thing is to leave it to the police. I mean that."

Tommy prodded a stained forefinger at him : " Take care of it myself first. When I finished with him the coppers can have him and welcome. He knocked my sister off, that's good enough for me and don't you give me any of that guff about the law taking its course. You been financing him so you know something about him : he never gave a woman a straight deal in his life and I know he was skint when my sister busted with him, she told me : soon as he gets a bit of cash he beats it. Don't that add up to something? Goes on the booze with my sister and creases her just like knocking off a rabbit—"

" All I can tell you," said Charles, " is that Warrender

L

is in this country, probably in London. He'll have a Humber Snipe Utility with him I think, a dark brown body with black wings."

"Know all about that," said Tommy. "I met the bloke who helped him fix it. I been moving round myself mister. That was the barrow you took on the fiddle with you, right?"

"You told the police all this?"

"They'll find out," said Tommy. "I dropped a little hint here and there. I don't like coppers. I can shovel up my own dirt. Go you scared, mister?"

Charles smiled. "Not in the way you think. There isn't much I can tell the police about Warrender that will help them in their investigation into your sister's death—I just met him off and on in London but he had scores of friends and acquaintances that I know nothing about. And I give you my word that I don't know where he is now."

Tommy looked at Isabella: "Is he giving it to me straight?"

She nodded. "If Warrender is a murderer we'll do everything we can to see he's caught and dealt with properly— and I have a private and personal reason for telling you that. Are the police looking for him now?"

"That's right, but I aim to get him first. It's kind of personal with me too. Maybe he didn't do it: I just want the chance of hearing him prove it to me, see?"

Tommy reached down and picked up the gauntlets on the carpet by his chair. He stood up. Angular, dangerous, chin out-thrust; twenty-two or three and his face still smooth; burning inside, ready for battle, his fingers twitching at his cigarette.

"If you hear a word from Warrender I want to know about it. Fast, see? As a private favour: but just make it quick." He was staring at Isabella. " I don't know what fiddle you been running between you with Warrender and I don't care, see? I know all about the way you had that Humber rigged—but I told you I don't like coppers. That make sense?"

" All right," said Charles. " It's a deal. How can we reach you?"

" I'll keep in touch," said Tommy flatly, " and this time you'll know what it's all about. Correct?" He nodded at them. " Night all." Then he strode out into the hall; in Tommy's circle you didn't see people out; they just left when they had enough.

The front door slammed, the motor-cycle barked twice outside the window and then roared off down the short drive and into the quiet avenue.

Isabella subsided into the nearest chair. " This rather alters things," she said.

" It does indeed," said John Connell. " That young man wasn't pretending."

" The point is, do we go to the police?" Charles said. " And if we do how much do we tell them? If they want Harry Warrender for murder they'll dig pretty deep and I wonder how long it will be before they come across us."

" You ought to talk to this Joachim Menendez," said John Connell. " How did you get on with him this evening?"

" Very well," Isabella said. " He's being most co-opera-tive now that he understand the full situation. Tomorrow night he expects to meet Warrender—we were planning to be there."

" If you take my advice," said John Connell, " you'll carry on as arranged : if you can get the paintings away from Warrender first you won't have wasted everything after all—then the police can deal with Warrender as they think fit. You're not shielding a suspected murderer because you don't in fact know where he is yet. If the meeting to-morrow night is a mess-up, that'll be different and the police could jump down your throats."

" There won't be any mess-up," Charles said. " Menendez and I can handle him. I bet he's hiding in some pub or shady hotel somewhere waiting to get his hands on thirty thousand pounds. You know, now that I think of it, I thought there was something wrong with Harry Warrender, especially on the drive down to Spain. He was all on edge and he made quite a business about getting an English newspaper—I thought it was nervousness about the trip, I even asked him once if he wanted to change his mind. And all the time it was that poor girl he was thinking about—"

Isabella shivered slightly and Charles put his arm around her waist. " I don't want you to come tomorrow night, darling," he said. " There won't be a fight, not with Menendez and myself giving him a surprise visit—"

" I'm coming," she said. " I have to. It's been my business from the start. Let's talk to Menendez."

Joachim Menendez listened to Isabella. A man who had killed a woman when she was drunk filled him with no kind of trepidation; he saw no reason to alter their arrangements for the following night and the police need know nothing about the paintings—in Joachim's colourful experience it was seldom a good thing to tell the police too much. The murder of the girl was a separate matter : they would make the police a present of the man they wanted. After-wards. Until tomorrow night, then—

17

Harry Warrender lay on the bed and watched the drifting smoke of his cigarette against the stained ceiling; he'd spent hours like that and the view didn't get any better. There was a bar downstairs and draught beer in goodish condition and customers ready with the cheery word; and last night there'd even been a woman, on her own, blonde, plump and genteel with a wandering eye. He had thought about it, he had thought about it more than a bit, but he hadn't done anything. Too much on his mind and women liked to yak, even casual pick-ups in bed.

There'd be plenty of time for that. Sophisticated stuff, smooth, perfumed, expensive—the best. It was going to be good . . . It was always good when you could buy the best—and with thirty thousand he was going to be able to keep himself. South America was the right bet, somewhere nice and sunny—loads of talent in little bathing suits on the beaches, nice long legs and all that loving waiting for him to stir it up. All he needed was the cash.

But he had to handle it right. Paris had been a mistake and the drain on his cash had been wicked. Hanging round the places and trying to work up the right contacts—it just couldn't be done in a hurry, not with stuff as valuable as the paintings; you needed good contacts and he hadn't had any at all—and the few people he'd tried had made him nervous.

Bringing the Humber back had been simple enough, but by that time Sandra was in the papers, and driving towards London had made him feel he was driving himself straight into the worst trouble in the world if he didn't watch his step; and even at thirty thousand the price might be too high if he finished up in jail.

Menendez had sounded all right from the very first, but he wasn't coming to Paris; Menendez didn't give a damn about the Mundayas and he had sounded as though he meant it and he talked the right language. He was sharp and he evidently didn't mind cutting a few corners, and that would make it all the simpler to deal with him.

A spatter of rain shook the window. Harry saw himself in the dressing-table mirror: he'd lost weight in the last week and he wasn't feeling in good shape; when he got out of this he'd have to take himself in hand; there was nothing wrong with him that the right supply of money couldn't cure—in the right company.

The real shaker had been seeing his name in the paper as a man the police were anxious to interview in connection with the body of the girl recently discovered in a water tank in the woods near Burnham. There hadn't been a picture, not yet; he had been described as about thirty-five years old, ruddy complexion, full face and with a heavy build—

He had already put a few lines out about getting a false passport and that had entailed seeing some people whom he would have preferred to avoid; the price was fifty pounds, payable in advance and that would take more than he had left, so it would have to wait until he had collected from Menendez.

Now that his name was in the papers it was going to be more difficult still. He had to get out of the country and they would be watching all the regular exits. Anyone who helped him get out was going to need money in advance and none of them would be cheap; he couldn't afford to slip now: the police would never believe his version of what had happened with Sandra—he had read every line that had been printed on the case and one of the tabloids had made quite a feature of the girl's name embroidered on the leg of her knickers.

Harry got up and looked out of the window to the streaming cobbled yard; there were four lock-up garages and the Humber was in one of them and he hadn't had it out since he had fetched up at the place four nights ago. He could hear the hoarse hooting of the river traffic; Woolwich had been as near into London as he had cared to go; he had signed himself in as Harold Walker and he had paid for a week in advance; nobody asked his business.

He stood for a long time watching the afternoon rain. There had been an indication of the way things might go that very morning. The Humber worried him: he knew Charles Connell and the girl were back—Menendez had admitted it and had said it didn't make any difference to him; all the same, if anything went wrong with the deal and he had to shift the Humber he would have felt happier if it wasn't so easily traced; so he had rung Striker Lewis from a call box and Striker hadn't wanted any part of him at all; so far from taking on a rush paint job on the Humber, Striker had made it clear that if Harry Warrender showed his face round the workshop again Striker would let him have it with a starting handle. So Harry hadn't strayed very far from his base.

Tonight he'd ring Menendez at ten, give him forty-five minutes to arrive and find the place, and meet him at the door into the yard; the pub would be shut and the landlord would be playing his nightly game of poker with his chosen few in his office behind the saloon bar; sometime in the course of the evening Harry would bring the pictures up to his bedroom so that Menendez could satisfy himself what he was getting—he had made a special point of it, that he'd want to check the pictures properly, and since Harry wasn't going to bring them to the Dorchester for inspection and Menendez refused to consider an open-air meeting the job would have to be done in the pub.

Handing over thirty thousand pounds for three valuable paintings that had travelled hundreds of miles in secret wasn't like buying an evening paper from the boy on the corner. " You trust me and I bring the money," Menendez had said. " If the goods are right I buy them. Yes?"

Harry drowsed through the afternoon, and he forced himself not to buy any more papers; it was a bad sign when a transient in a dingy pub littered his bedroom with newspapers and went out very seldom—and then on foot when he had a large powerful car waiting in the garage.

The waiting was hell. There was so much that he had to shut his mind to and not think about—Sandra, and Charles Connell and that old fool Luis Mundaya sprawling in the archway—some of it still made him sweat when it slipped into his mind last thing at night. It would be different when he had the money in his hand. Money changed everything.

When the bar opened he made himself go out for a walk; he could do his drinking afterwards and by God he would; the rain had stopped and there were people about; he found his way down to the ferry and he spent a long time leaning against an iron chain, smoking and looking at the dirty water and the ships moving down and he had a sudden conviction that it was going to be all right for him after tonight; he'd fix that passport, get out of London up to Liverpool or Glasgow and keep himself pretty quiet until things were easier. And then get himself a sea passage.

He walked past a couple of young policemen and they didn't give him a second glance. He took a bus ride to Charlton and walked up over Blackheath and he felt so right that he called in at a pub and had some food and beer, a little beer carefully drunk.

At ten o'clock he was in a call box giving Joachim Menendez directions; Menendez said he would drive himself and the money would be with him; he was to use the side door into the yard by the garages; he understood perfectly.

He knelt on the bed by the window; his room was in darkness and by the street lamp further up he could watch the turning and the yard; he had the gun in the side pocket of his jacket; Joachim Menendez might try to be smart; he sounded sharp enough. The three paintings, still in their wrapping, stood against the wall.

It was just ten minutes to eleven when a yellow and black Rolls Royce turned slowly in and stopped. The driver got out and in the light from the street lamp his loose grey suit looked almost white; he was a bigger man than Harry had expected; he reached into the car and brought out a wide-brimmed grey hat and a suitcase. Harry scrambled off the bed, drew the curtains, and put on the light. The sight of that opulent Rolls had cheered him nearly as much as the suitcase.

He met Menendez by the side door and they had no greeting. Harry went upstairs first and into his room.

Menendez took off his hat politely and dropped his suitcase on the bed. Harry could hardly drag his gaze from it.

"There they are," he said. "Just the way they were packed."

"You permit?" Without waiting for any answer Menendez took up one of the pictures. A small penknife had appeared in his hand. Very carefully he slit the folds of sacking and drew the picture out. It was the portrait of a woman, head and shoulders; a long melancholy face with deep eyes and a small pursed-up mouth. Menendez gave it a very quick look and his expression showed nothing. In the same way he undid the other two: each was a portrait of the same woman, but the set of her head had changed and the pursed-up mouth had loosened into a tiny secret smile.

"They're all right," said Harry Warrender, "aren't they? They're what you expected?" He couldn't keep the shaking out of his voice.

Menendez ignored him. He had all three pictures free of their coverings now; two he placed flat on the dressing-table, the third he began to examine with a small glass, inch by inch; he moved the tip of one finger delicately over the brush-work, tilting the picture and checking it from all angles; he gave the back of the canvas a most minute inspection. And he went through the same process with the other two. Harry lit a cigarette and when he offered one to Menendez all he got was a muttered: "I have more important things—"

Harry wanted to shout at him to get on with it. The pictures were all right. The minutes crawled by and Menendez seemed to be getting slower and slower and more deliberate still; frowning, his lower lip thrust out, balancing the frames in his hand, his eyes half-closed.

Harry felt the sudden sweat in the small of his back as he

looked at that case on the bed. Thirty thousand in fivers. It made his hands shake.

Menendez ranged the three pictures side by side, squatting and propping them against the wall. Then he straightened up and stood back.

" Yes," he said softly.

" They're all right, aren't they all right?" Warrender's voice was quick and hoarse and eager.

Menendez was standing beside him, smiling a little, so Harry Warrender knew it was all right.

" Three paintings of the same lovely sad lady," said Menendez. " A high-born Spanish lady and who knows what her sorrows were all those years ago, my friend? See, the last painting shows her with the smile beginning—so sweet, so tender. Nobody has ever found out who she was or why Zurbaran painted her—it is the three paintings together that give them the value for the collector, such as myself : always they must be together." He shifted his cuff back and looked at his watch; its jewelled case glittered in the light, and his cuff links were blood red rubies against the whiteness of his shirt.

Harry Warrender relaxed. " That's fine," he said. " They're all yours."

Menendez went over to the window and pulled the curtain aside. And when he turned back there was a small gun in his hand. He was no longer a slightly comic wealthy South American with an ostentatious car and too much jewellery. He moved up and halted in front of Harry Warrender.

" The hands on the back of your head, my friend, and then turn around. I am taking the gun you carry in your pocket."

Harry Warrender swore, lifting his hands.

"And to your mother and sister," said Menendez. "Turn. It will make little noise for me to shoot you in the belly."

Harry Warrender turned around and his gun was removed. Something like this had been in the back of his mind. And now he was letting it happen to him. He was shaking with anger. He heard something thump on the floor behind him.

"You can look, but be careful."

He turned. The suitcase lay at his feet. It was open and it was quite empty.

"You have surprise in your face," said Menendez softly. "You think I will help you to steal from Señorita Isabella Mundaya? I, Joachim Menendez whose family found it an honour to serve the Mundayas? No, my friend, this is one thing I cannot do ever."

"You've got the pictures," said Warrender desperately. "At least pay me a percentage—don't grab the lot! Listen, I'll settle for five thousand! I brought them here for you —you owe me something!"

"You dishonour me." Joachim Menendez was smiling quite unpleasantly and his eyes had a hardness that told Harry Warrender that little gun in his hand had been used before; it was no new experience to Joachim Menendez to have a loser pleading with him. "If I pay you what is owed to you, my friend, you are a dead man very soon. Do you forget Luis Mundaya who is now in his grave? Or a man who was your friend and who gave you trust?"

Harry Warrender shook his head. "That was different—"

The door opened and Charles Connell came in.

"My God," said Harry Warrender bitterly, "so you've finally fixed this all right!"

"I hope so," said Charles. "Forgive me if I don't find

your present position very enviable—was it worth it, Harry? Tell me, did you have something like this in your mind from the start?"

"I'm not crying," said Harry Warrender. "I just lost."

"How right you are." Charles Connell went over, keeping away from the gun, and stacked the pictures together. He knew he shouldn't try to lift them. But he knew also the way Harry Warrender would be watching him. So he got his arms around them, holding them against his chest.

There was some sort of movement going on by the stairs. Feet pounding. Isabella was down below, waiting, but this wasn't Isabella coming up the stairs in a hurry.

Menendez shifted his attention. Warrender kicked the open suitcase so that it hit Menendez in the shins. And Warrender darted forward and grabbed at the gun. The two heavy men blundered about the room, heaving and straining and grunting. They hit the bed and then rolled on the floor and Warrender was on top for a moment and then Menendez rolled him over and rammed the top of his head again and again into Warrender's face.

Tommy stood and watched from the door; behind him his two fair-haired assistants. The scene met with Tommy's approval, up to a point. Warrender was getting a bashing. That was all right. But Tommy intended to do the bashing. He said something over his shoulder. And the three of them moved in.

Joachim Menendez was prised off his victim and Tommy patted him on the shoulder and said:

"You done all right, mister. Now it's for us. See?"

Joachim Menendez straightened his clothes. He didn't see it at all.

"They want him," Charles said, "rather more urgently than we do."

Tommy looked at Charles. "You never told me he was here. We had to follow you."

"At least one of you has been following me all day," Charles said. "When you rang this evening I did give you a hint that I'd be going out shortly after ten o'clock— I knew you were behind, but my friend here needed to have the first little talk with Warrender. You make a fairly conspicuous trio, and on those bikes you couldn't lose us."

Harry Warrender had backed against the wall; his nose was bleeding and he was breathing loudly through his open mouth.

"Charles!" he whispered, "for God's sake don't leave me with them!"

With the six of them in the room it was crowded. Tommy had Joachim Menendez's gun. Now he gave it back to him.

"Beat it," he said. "The both of you. This is private."

Charles nodded at Joachim Menendez over the top edge of the pictures. "We'd better. Help me with these."

Only Harry Warrender watched their departure and Charles didn't look back. There was no sound in the room as the door closed. The barmaid had reached her bedroom overhead and she had her radio now turned to full volume.

Isabella met them in the yard. "No trouble," said Charles quietly. "At least not for us."

They put the pictures very carefully on the wide back seat of the Rolls. "Tomorrow," said Joachim Menendez, "you will take lunch with me, please, and we will finish this business between us."

Isabella smiled in the light from the street lamp. "It's really over?" she murmured.

Charles looked at the lock-up garages. The Humber would be in one of them. Two were empty, their doors propped back. He could see no reason to make a present of the Humber to anybody, not even Harry Warrender, though he doubted whether Harry Warrender would be doing any driving for a long time.

Joachim Menendez opened his magnificent tool kit. He had everything. They forced a padlock, pulled the doors back. And there was the Humber. Charles reversed it out and turned. Behind that curtained window up there things would be happening to Harry Warrender.

Isabella drove the Rover and he followed and they stopped at a telephone kiosk. Charles dialled 999 Police and that if they wanted to find Harry Warrender they'd have to hurry. He quoted the name of the pub and rang off, and privately he was hoping that Tommy and his two colleagues would have left before the police arrived. They parted company with the black and yellow Rolls and drove through the southern suburbs.

When they reached Weybridge John Connell was waiting for them. He said Tommy had been on the phone twenty minutes before.

"He sounded almost happy," said John Connell, "but he said he'd like to meet the geezer who called the coppers: they got away with only a minute or so in hand."

The papers the next morning reported that Harry Warrender had been taken into custody the night before; he was being detained in the prison hospital and it was understood that it might be some time before he would be fit to be brought before a magistrate. The charge was murder. There was no mention of the real circumstances of the arrest.

They met Joachim Menendez in his suite at the Dorchester before lunch. He announced that he was happy to be keeping his word: the paintings were in excellent condition and had taken no harm from their unorthodox journeyings. The price was going to be thirty-five thousand and he was getting the bargain of his life, he freely admitted it.

They stood in front of the three portraits—the soft depth of colour and the subtle warmth that grew into the sad face in the third portrait, those deep dark eyes in the pale austere face with a hint of white teeth as the smile was breaking through.

"The Spanish Lady," said Joachim Menendez softly. "See, she is smiling for us again."

But Charles Connell had eyes only for the bright-haired girl who stood so quietly beside him, her hand resting lightly on his arm. And when she looked up and smiled at him it had a radiance beyond all the compass of art. "Beautiful," he said. And even Joachim Menendez knew how right he was.